PERFECT TENSE

Michael Bracewell was born in 1958. The author of two novellas, three novels and a study of English culture, *England is Mine*, he writes regularly on music, art and literature for the *Independent on Sunday* and *Frieze* magazine.

Michael Bracewell

PERFECT TENSE

VINTAGE

Published by Vintage 2002

2 4 6 8 10 9 7 5 3 1

First published in Great Britain 2001 by
Jonathan Cape

Vintage
The Random House Group Limited
20 Vauxhall Bridge Road, London SW1V 2SA

Random House Australia (Pty) Limited
20 Alfred Street, Milsons Point, Sydney,
New South Wales 2061, Australia

Random House New Zealand Limited
18 Poland Road, Glenfield,
Auckland 10, New Zealand

Random House (Pty) Limited
Endulini, 5a Jubilee Road, Parktown 2193, South Africa

The Random House Group Limited Reg. No. 954009

www.randomhouse.co.uk

A CIP catalogue record for this book
is available from the British Library

ISBN 0 099 44065 2

Papers used by Random House are natural,
recyclable products made from wood grown in sustain-
able forests. The manufacturing processes conform to the
environmental regulations of the country of origin.

Printed and bound in Denmark by
Nørhaven Paperback A/S, Viborg

Perfect Tense

ONE

Work is a blessing. I keep repeating this to myself, whenever I feel like chucking the whole thing in. Because worse than work, far worse, is not working. And I'm not just talking about the people who sleep in parks, or the people who get laid off when they've got a family to feed. I'm talking about the rest of us, the ones with jobs and wages, who still manage to spend half of the time wishing that we could blow the whole caboodle sky high, and the other half simply feeling tired.

Of course, I'm thinking of people with jobs like mine: the stragglers in the race of an office career, disqualified from the fast track by our fundamental lack of interest in winning. But even then, work is a blessing. I say this — just on the wrong side of forty — because work, ultimately, is the one thing that keeps the rest in place. It's difficult to show you what I mean — unless you share my dread of public holidays.

On public holidays, I like to go for long walks around the quiet streets of the City, looking at the empty offices and peering through the windows of the darkened, scrubbed-down coffee bars. I know it sounds ridiculous, but I find them reassuring – those frontages of mirrored glass, and the reception desks with their bored security men, dozing in high-backed leather chairs. These are the sights which keep my fear of redundancy at bay. Because it's easy to feel redundant, even when you're harnessed to the office and perfectly aware of all the other poor sods who really have lost their jobs. Redundacy can be a feeling in your head as well. It's the feeling of having nowhere to go – or, 'nowhere to go but indoors', as someone once put it. And I can't think of a better definition. To feel that bored, and that irrelevant; to be adrift, and no longer connected to life, so that nothing – neither effort nor reward – can justify your getting up or sleeping. And it can happen when you least expect it.

You might be wondering who I am, or what I look like. It doesn't matter. You wouldn't look twice if you saw me on the train. I look just like everyone else. And I suppose that I am just like everyone else, when you get down to it. But I ought to say 'male, white, British'. And you could add 'white-collar-low-to-middle-income-bracket-suburban-but-has-read-a-few-books' if you wanted.

But once, nearly twenty years ago, back in the summer of 1980, I was on my way to the office when I suddenly decided to bunk off for the day. It was early June, a cloudless morning, and the sun was already hot. I was walking over London Bridge – back in those days I was working near the Monument, and I used to walk over the bridge every day, from the station – and I was looking at the sunlight on the river.

When I narrowed my eyes so that they were nearly closed, the glints of light on the water became a single sparkling mass, dazzling white, flickering on black. And when I tried to look ahead again, the glare of the sunshine was so bright that I had to stare down at the pavement as I walked along. All around me, the workers were streaming in to the City. I was always fascinated by the different speeds at which they walked. Their lives were in their walks, if you know what I mean. Some strolled, disdainful of a rush which questioned their status, or demonstrating an ease which seemed distinctly continental; others hurried at a frantic pace, their jackets over one arm and the sweat on their shoulders already making their shirts stick to their backs. These were the ones who sometimes talked to themselves as they rushed along, as though they were rehearsing their defence for some accusation which was going to be hurled at them the moment they got into the office.

Then there were those who actually marched over the bridge: the officer class of the old guard, the umbrella-tappers who bore themselves erect, staring ahead with watery eyes which seemed to reveal only the dullest intelligence, but conveyed an air of complete disapproval of anything which didn't belong to their world.

But what was their world? They were a dying breed,

dinosaurs even then, and soon their City – the City of tailcoats and wing collars almost – would be buried for good beneath the new generation of radical architecture and lean young men with American qualifications and Swiss passports. And yet the idea of this old guard would linger, in the furnishings of wine bars and those dark, busy little shops where men with silver hair sold hand-made shirts to graduates with toned bodies and fat pens. But it was only the idea of the old guard that remained; and that was the factor – it seemed more like a process – which interested me. That here would be a crumbling chunk of history which would remain present in a feeble dilution of its ambience, like those new pubs on old City sites where they keep a fragment of medieval masonry on display behind a sheet of perspex which is soon covered in greasy thumb prints.

Not that I could give a toss about medieval masonry, or the old guard of the City for that matter. No, what held my attention was the fact that I was witnessing a time when most things, including hard cash and our perception of reality itself, were about to be turned into an idea of themselves. Perhaps it has always been that way, but some time around the early Eighties I began to notice the insistence of image over substance. And this insistence began to pester me, like a bad radio station that you can't turn off. And now I find I still can't turn it off.

Anyway, getting back to that morning in early June;

there I was, walking over London Bridge and looking at the buildings as they seemed to absorb the light, and I knew that the sky would turn a deeper and deeper shade of blue as the day wore on. And I don't know why, but there seemed to be something ancient, and monolithic, about the sides of those high buildings as they faced the glare of the sun.

And so I stopped and looked some more: at the jewels of light on the surface of the river and at the brooding, imperial edifice of the City.

The day seemed to urge adventure, whispering the promise from some mysterious side street that exploration would find its reward, by evening, of an extraordinary experience; that with dusk, when the clearing streets were soft and grey, I would have found a treasure which made the City, and everything in it or of it, my own. I had only to search.

Slightly drunk with the thought that I was actually going to step off the treadmill, I stood for a moment longer on the bridge. I could feel the ascending sun hot on the back of my head as I wavered in a sudden crowd of choices. I have always been incapable of making quick decisions, as more than one line manager has written on my annual assessment form, and the decision of what to do with a stolen day of freedom – following so fast on the initial decision not to go into the office – was all but too much for me. But I also felt that I had been challenged by the City, or by the whole of London, not simply to be worthy of its complexity, depth and grandeur, but also (in my arrogance) to prove my spiritual superiority over my fellow workers, who even now were heading towards their allotted offices with the expression, serene or anxious, of those who start their day a little late.

I was an outlaw already: a criminal who was contemptuous, even, of the lassitude offered by flexitime. With each passing minute, as I plunged through the undergrowth of that forbidden territory which flanks the straight and narrow path of core office hours, I was accumulating a responsibility to my crime which would be the first test of my endurance. Soon, the sensation of drunkenness had given way to a thick-headed feeling of concussion, accompanied by an actual dizziness which I could only attribute to the warmth of the sun, or nerves. The edges of my peripheral vision began to darken. I thought that I was either going to faint or throw up. I moved to one side of the pavement and leaned against the smooth stone of the balustrade, my hands pressing lightly upon it. Steadying myself, and catching just the lightest breeze off the river, my head began to clear. But I seized almost gratefully on my sudden dead drop into nausea. I would have to find a telephone box and phone in sick.

Because I had my back to the passing workers I began to feel conspicuous, and so I turned around again, this time being careful not to catch anyone's eye, and look as though I was taking the time to judge them. This was not a location, at that time of day, in which it was usual to be stationary; and I attracted a succession of sideways glances, none of which were accusatory in themselves, but all of which – because of their very brevity and apparent indifference – seemed to be saying, 'We've met your type before, and we haven't got the time, or the interest, frankly, to get involved with whatever little mess of deceit you might be concocting so as not to go into the office. And by the way, if you're not with us, then you're against us.'

But it wasn't – it isn't – a question of being either for or against my fellow workers. For as long as I can remember, I have had an equal mistrust of organized authority and organized rebellion – of obedience to conformity and obedience to non-conformity. I'm inclined towards aspects of both, but I seem to have a reflex which tends towards the opposite of any given orthodoxy. Show me a strutting rebel and I'll want to be a humourless bourgeois; sit me in a room filled with high-powered executives and I'll probably yawn in their faces. Is this so odd, I wonder?

For me it is simply a feeling of being out of step, which is maybe quite common, and certainly apparent in certain members of my generation who were born in the late Fifties and early Sixties. We opened our eyes to asphalt in the twilight of austerity; we were too young to experience the bright new worlds of agitation and liberation which shaped the lives of our elder siblings; and, to be honest with you, all I can remember of the Eastern Utopia of freak power — as it arrived in south London, at any rate — is a strong smell of sackcloth and damp wicker baskets. A smell which seemed to define what I imagined to be the audience at free festivals, where girls in long skirts rolled carefully assembled joints with the same attention to detail that their great-grandmothers most probably applied to embroidery samplers; and beside these girls, young men with lank hair, thick sideburns, and child-like faces. All beneath a bone-white sky.

Then again, we were just that bit too old to buy into the rumble of a world described by advertising and products. If we didn't want to get back to the land, then neither did we trust the rhetoric of retail. That was the world where everything had turned into an idea of itself, where life no longer had an inner life.

If there is a distinguishing characteristic of the latest commodified, high-on-themselves generation of cultural materialists, then it's the habit they all have of speaking in a tone of voice which turns their statements into questions. That reflex of making a sentence rise up at its end, as though to coerce agreement in advance, rather than proving a point. It seems to stand for the triumph of self-obsession, the other badge of which is the need to be yabbering into a mobile phone all the time.

And this all seems connected to that moment when

image became insistent, and when everything turned into its received idea. It's a process which just seems to have built up, like an accumulation of fat around the heart's weary muscle. But what do I know? Most younger people all seem to know exactly where they're going and exactly how much it's worth.

So what did we believe in – the generation who were out of step? I think that we were guided most by a deep sense of anxiety – you could almost describe it as sub-sonic; and then, perhaps as a consequence of that, we were hopelessly, socially awkward: always trying to move away from whoever was trying to make us join in with something. And yet we kicked off innocent, open to empathy and filled with compassion. So why then did compassion curdle and find its way to bitterness?

Perhaps it would be more accurate to describe us – the awkward generation – as having been forced open at a formative age by some degree of wounding. Not, necessarily, that we have staggered through our lives in pain. Rather, we rose and fell on the thermal currents of our emotions: trying on masks, seeking out addictions, or addicts, looking for gurus and turning time and again to romance. And when all of that had failed, we settled for protection on the best terms we could find it – 'superfluous men', to borrow a Russian phrase.

It all goes back to decisions made during adolescence, I think. When we finally ventured out of the house, our stooped shoulders and self-mocking, fashion-mocking fashions were eloquent of a particular sort of loneliness. This was the solitude of the adolescent's bedroom, the width of a wall from Mum and Dad, but housing a private kingdom in which we had created our secret selves for a battle with the outside world which was never fully engaged.

In our minds, we had trained on the gyratory of hatred, embarrassment and awkwardness; we were the big girls' blouses on whom the football teacher had let loose his ridicule. We became autofacts — 'self-created', in an anti-style which performed a commentary on itself: 'Miss Haversham in male drag', stood up at the altar by society in general (or so we liked to think) and now bulimic on the stale icing of adversarial poetry. On such a diet we tried going out at night and always seemed to wind up waiting on empty platforms.

This dandyism of our youth — which mocked the sombre teacher and the tough delinquent alike — seemed only to hatch a disaffection through which we subscribed to a premature sense of futility; and from there we turned Puritan, bitter and parched, concluding that we hated the world because we'd found no place within it.

What was known as punk rock could only exist for a fleeting few months of cartoon anarchy; and of all the people I knew from those months — who spiked their hair with K Y jelly, or got arrested for stealing coat-hangers

out of dustbins, or who spat at bass guitarists and missed
– they have all acted out the Three Ps of punk, to
become pig farmers, postmen or psychiatric nurses;
the rest have found a fourth and passed away.

And so I wasn't for or against the other office
workers who glanced at me, as I hesitated that summer
morning on London Bridge. I was simply out of step.
This much was brought home to me as I joined the
remainder of the commuters who were striding, strolling
or strutting over the bridge. I began to feel hotter
than ever, but this time with the sense of fraudu-
lence which accompanied my inclusion within that elite
band who were clearly allowed to keep their own
hours.

There is a particular sort of panic for the lower
order of office worker which sets in when he or she
has just become officially unaccounted for within the
office. It is more than just a sense of guilt – in fact,
guilt itself hardly ever comes into it; rather, it is the
high octane formula of anticipation which derives from
the swiftly accumulating weight of explanation, lies and
excuses which they start to rehearse in their heads.
Because with each lie or excuse or explanation you
are forced to give away a little bit more of your
private self at the office. And it is the private self
– the unknown self – which armours your dignity
and maintains your independence, on those bad days
when you feel as though your life has become a brown

carpet tile, sticky and reeking with spilled coffee from the vending machine.

I am superstitious about telephone boxes, sometimes making awkward detours just to make my call from a particular booth that I believe will in some way be favourable to the outcome of that call. This is largely a question of atmosphere and loyalty to the sites of pleasant memories. Off Oxford Street, for example, there is a narrow cut through to Eastcastle Street which has the benefit of always seeming secluded and quiet. Widening at its northern end, where the studios and showrooms of milliners and drapers make their own busy enclave, this passage possesses no features other than the back door to a pub – where a row of empty steel kegs, pungent with the smell of stale beer, can usually be seen – and a line of telephone boxes, five in all, pressed hard against the glistening brick of a three-storey building.

In times of crisis, when just the thought of making a telephone call has been enough to bring a stabbing sensation of tightness just beneath my sternum, I have often turned to this location in order to call on a calm which the sites of certain other telephone boxes – the unscreened, brutal clamour of the booths facing Centre Point, for example – would be incapable of delivering. Whenever I am in a telephone box, I become acutely aware of its surrounding ambience, as though the booth were part of some stark theatre set – placed stage left, for example, and lit by one dimmed spot which casts the rest of the scenery into shadow and brings out the yawning darkness of the wings in a way which is more forlorn than ominous. From this you can tell that I seem to have developed an exaggerated softness to the impact of my days.

But on the particular occasion which I was recounting, back in the early summer of 1980, I made my way to a brace of unfrequented telephone boxes which I had noticed at the entrance to an alley which led off Upper Thames Street. Here, more or less in the shadow of London Bridge, I had the impression of being at the foot of a white cliff, alone with a wheeling of gulls which would be little more than specks in the dazzling blue sky. I remember this alley as being cut in two by shadow; the morning sunshine caught on the soot-blackened bricks of the facing wall with a clarity which gave minuscule shadows to even the stamen-like fur on the moss that was growing between them.

The heavy door of the telephone box, hinged on canvas straps, would only yield to a determined tug. Once inside, I began to rehearse my excuses to the office. The classically simple, 'I've got to the station and I feel really sick' underpinned its faked veracity by virtue of being spoken from a phone box; but there is a general weakness about the actual excuse

– '. . . and I feel really sick' – which, when coming from a clerical level, somehow rides the back-curve of credibility. Anyone from a line manager upwards might get away with it, but coming from a drone . . . But I couldn't think of anything better, and the day was calling me on.

It has become a truism that most telephone boxes smell of human urine, but in the case of my own chosen box that morning tradition had outdone itself to provide not only the odour of urine, but also, neat in one corner, a compact, tubular piece of human faeces. I had already dialled the area code for my line manager's office before I noticed it, and recognition led me to falter.

Given the location of the excrement, it was difficult to calculate where its donor must have squatted – unless it had simply been placed there, like a landmine, by minds set on devilment; and I was conscious of this conundrum even as I continued to dial, with automatic hand, the number of Fat Val's shabby, ivory-coloured telephone. The number connected, giving way to the short, asthmatic rasps of its ringing tone.

Everyone thought that Fat Val, the line manager, was also mad. But both her cruel nickname and this popular belief were a shade wide of the bull's-eye. She was one of those people who lowers everyone's spirits the moment they walk in to the room – and maybe she knew it. Squat and broad-shouldered, her wide features were flushed with patches of a dry rash which seemed to indicate either allergies or a surfeit of niacin. As soon as she got to work she would change her shoes for a pair of wooden-soled flip-flops, the slapping sound of which, as she trailed across the office with a file in one hand and a fag in the other, would somehow seem to make the time pass even more slowly. And this, you could tell, made people dislike her.

Dressed in a shapeless, round-necked pullover and a thin, knee-length cotton skirt, she wore her straight hair (which was the colour of damp corn) pulled back from her forehead in a viciously tight top-knot, which was bound at its stem by a pair of elastic bands from the stationery cupboard. Looking at the roots of her fringe, tugged back so severely from the reddened skin just beneath her hairline, it used to make my eyes water just imagining the strain on her scalp.

Although she was only in her middle thirties. Fat Val moved around the office with a heaviness and ill-temper which suggested a lifetime of suffering. Not that she moved around that much: mostly, she just sat behind her desk and sighed, short exhalations between her pursed lips, which sometimes turned into low, quiet groans, and which gave a running commentary on her soul-crushing weariness. You were always waiting for something to snap.

How can I describe Waste, the office over which

Fat Val presided and my first proper office job? It was a department that cleared foreign currencies for the Overseas Division of a granite and marble British bank, but this description, as with so much in office life at a certain level, makes Waste sound far grander than it really was.

The office itself was little more than the back rooms of one floor of a massive, ornate Edwardian building, which had its main entrance — replete with polished brass, Ionic columns and liveried doorman — on Eastcheap, but which we were only allowed to enter through a side door. This entrance led into an annex, built in the middle of the 1960s, on the corner of Fish Street Hill.

Everything about this annex, and our entrance to the office, seemed to be connected to the colour brown. On the ground floor, the street-facing windows were tinted brown, and the stiff net curtains which covered them were brown with the dust and the dirt which blew out through the brown grilles on the air-conditioning units which ran along their length; the carpet tiles in the reception area were brown, as were the doors to the lift, and the whole place seemed to smell as dried out, musty and airless as the corrugated cardboard boxes which were usually waiting to be thrown out beside the dark staircase which flanked the liftshaft.

The liftshaft and the stairwell occupied their own tower, with an oblong window — the panes brown with the outlines of dried, dirty raindrops — on each of its six landings. The metal frames of these windows had been thickened by many coats of off-white enamel paint. As you made your way up to Waste — which was on the first floor and not worth the exasperation of waiting for the lift — you could hear the machinery in the liftshaft clanking and thudding, and watch, through its metal cage, the tightening and raising of the oiled black cables.

In the afternoons this stairwell caught the setting sun and the darkness of each landing would be broken up by vivid stretched squares of amber-coloured light. You have to remember that this was at a time when most offices were still largely mechanical; even though the age of computers was approaching — that great evolutionary jolt in the rise of Organization Man — there remained the stolid atmosphere of cumbersome adding machines and dusty piles of ledgers.

Back in those days, there were all kinds of arcane items of office equipment — odd-looking keyboards attached to complicated systems of levers, wheels and rods, which seemed to have keepers rather than technicians. Officially supplied in the drawer of every metal desk was a tin-foil ashtray and nearly everyone smoked; young clerks still took their fifteen minute morning coffee breaks in the dim basement of the old Kardomah Café on Eastcheap, even though their heads might have been filled with the first eerie elegies of robotic synthesizer music.

In front of the double swing doors which led into the main two offices of Waste, there was a strip of brown carpet which had been worn down to the rubber of its underlay by the constant rushing and jostling of the clerks, to say nothing of the huge plastic boxes of dead files and papers which the porters dragged through on a more or less hourly basis. The doors themselves were kicked and scuffed, and there was a heavy boot print, at waist height, for all the time that I worked there.

These offices were, I suppose, a version of what Honoré de Balzac called 'the bank's kitchen' — the scullery of finance, where all pretence at professional nicety or gravitas would be laughed out of the building. Actually, part classroom, part shop-floor and part abandoned office space, Waste was more like the sewage farm of finance than anything else, a few steps down the food chain, in fact, from Balzac's 'bank's kitchen'.

If you could have the atmosphere of a sub-basement on a first floor, then Waste had it. Even though the two big offices had long windows running down the length of one wall, the glare through which on a summer morning would give you a sick headache in a matter of minutes, the feel of the place was stark and forlorn. In one half of the office there were the four long benches on which we carried out most of our clerical tasks; in the other there was an assortment of machines which processed, counted and encoded slips of paper. To any new arrival, the sight of these machines was formidable – they looked like hybrids of typewriters and looms – and dire fables were passed around about old so-and-so who nearly went the way of all flesh by getting his tie caught up in the works.

At Waste, new employees of the bank would find that they had sunk like human sediment from the shining surface waters of Personnel, some five floors above. I remember how, on my first morning, the matronly Mrs Doughty from Staff Contracts had finally delivered me to the shabby premises of Waste; and how, with each diminution of furnishings and decoration, as we descended from the seductive plush of her own cosy department – all rubber plants and oatmeal sofas – to these lower regions of dented filing cabinets and cramped corridors, there was an uneasy silence between us as though I had just become the victim of an elaborate confidence trick, the trap of which had been honeyed with her smooth talk of careers and promotions.

Waste was staffed, at a clerical level, by school leavers from East London; the boys, for the most part, were cocky and sharp-witted, while the girls all seemed too bored to speak. It was our job, every day, to count up the values of thousands of foreign cheques, and to run them through the encoding machines which would stamp each cheque with the bank's own clearing number. And at the end of each banking day, Waste was supposed to produce a grand total for the cleared and encoded currencies which would tally with another figure — delivered from powers as remote to us as a brigadier is to a squaddie. Three times out of five, when Fat Val groaned out the day's target figure to the hushed and expectant office — because if we were right we could start packing up to go home — we would discover that we were several hundred pounds, or even a couple of million, out of line in our calculations. And, as our daily task was nothing more than adding up figures and stamping cheques, there was nothing for it but to go through the whole lot again, trying to pick up dropped figures and tease out subtle combinations of reversed digits (caused by the numerical dyslexia that comes with spending four hours on a mechanical adding machine) which, when realigned, would magically iron out our mistake.

On the days when we were 'out', the individual reactions of the twenty or so of us who worked on this fiscal assembly line would tell you a lot about their individual characters, and about the attitude of the office in general. Fat Val, leaning against the door of the glass-sided cubicle which served as her private sanctum in the corner of the office, would barely have finished announcing the astronomically high figure of the day's foreign total before a tremendous shout of exasperation, rage and despair would erupt from us drones at the first wrong digit — which meant, of course, that the total figure was wrong. It had all the emotion of today's Lottery announcements only with the reverse emotions.

This collective uproar was usually led by Luke, a portly young man whose bellow of 'Cunting bollocks!' could have dominated a football terrace, and whose voluptuous, full-lipped girlfriend, Sally, who also worked in our office, would always give him a look of long-suffering disgust at his public display of foul language. To which Luke, in his turn, would react with a gape of injured innocence before looking around the office for support, with outstretched arms and wide, incredulous eyes.

Then, Fat Val would stomp back into her little office, too disgusted and weary to do anything. Before her would lie a formidable print-out, the thickness of a telephone directory, on the sharp-edged, pale blue pages of which, somewhere amidst the thousands of printed numbers that were barely legible, would lurk the solution to our common problem. It was rather as though we were caught up in the labours of a classical myth, and that Fat Val was trapped in the web of some curse in a fairy tale; it always seemed to me, as we dragged, hurled or applied ourselves to the business of trawling back through the day's figures, that we were going to be there for a year and a day.

I can remember most of the people with whom I have worked in various offices, over the years: a legion of Pauls and Steves and Pams, friendly for the most part, but brought back to mind transparent, like mist or a fading fax, and unsmiling. Other than Luke and Fat Val, there were two people in Waste who made a deep impression on me, and these were Les and Martin.

In every way, these two young men were the opposite of one another, beginning with the fact that Les looked like an effeminate Mexican and Martin was more or less albino. Les was tall and dapper. His black hair, which was always stiff with lacquer, was combed in a high wave over his head and cut to reveal just the lobes of his ears. It was like a helmet of hair, from the bulge of the swept-back fringe at the front to the heavy line of the cut across the collar at the back – a 'Boston' back, in fact; and Les's narrow brown head, with its almond-shaped eyes the colour of espresso coffee, and his long nose underlined by what used to be called a 'Zapata' moustache, always looked as though it would move independently of his helmet of lacquered hair – in the comic tradition of loose toupees. Les was by far and away the most elegant of the young men in Waste: a cubist arrangement of greens and browns, at severe angles to each other. His moss green trousers had a razor crease running down from their front pleats, and his chocolate brown shirts were always freshly ironed from collar to tail. He wore double cuffs, with outrageous silver links which were set with polished amethysts or some smooth brown stone called a tiger's eye, which looked like a buffed humbug. His thin-soled shoes were myriad, from snakeskin pumps the colour of jellied eels to little black patent leather dress shoes with a tiny gold chain across their instep.

But it was Les's ties that were the signature, so to speak, on his masterpiece of autofaction. Always wide-knotted, in a neat, fat lozenge of satin between the rounded collars of his brown shirt, they would change in colour from day to day to cover most shades from mushroom to claret. Some were embroidered with starbursts of silken thread, while others bore muted kaleidoscopes of navy blue shadows. He looked like a Latin American dictator disguised as the crooner on a cruise liner.

As offices abound with more myths and legends than the European vision of the Old West, so it was rumoured in Waste that Les could tot up a wad of foreign cheques using just his wetted finger and a staggering capacity for mental arithmetic. On the days when we were out, and down to our last hope of finding our mistake, word would spead around the office that Les was going to do one last count. And then we would all gather to watch the performance, for Les was essentially a performer, and we his audience, whatever role he chose. First, we were daunted, honest citizens, huddled along the raised walkways of Main Street to watch the elegant marshal taking out the one-eyed killer. Then Les would perform more like a sushi chef, with his long tapering fingers a blur of digital dexterity as he cut through the chaos of raw figures with the surgical accuracy of cold steel. Finally, when he had found the rogue cheque, he would throw back his head in a last dramatic flourish of triumph and exhaustion – all but looking for his seconds to throw a cape around his shoulders, or a junior member of the ballet school to present him with a bunch of long-stemmed roses. Martin called him a big poof.

As Les was dark and Martin albino, so their answering of one another's appearance and temperament, point for point as direct opposites, extended to the last detail. Les, with regard to his position in the office hierarchy, was a kind of bosun between Fat Val and ourselves. Flitting between the line manager's over-heated little cubicle and the main offices of Waste, with an expression on his face which always seemed to suggest that he knew far more than he was letting on, Les would relay unwelcome orders in a language that we wary young clerks would understand; and you can be sure that he was always careful to infer that he was just as put upon as the rest of us – united with us in our suffering.

Arguing the latest command from Fat Val to a mili-tant drone such as Luke – who would face him, hands on hip, with an expression of recalcitrant obstinacy – Les would lower his voice to an urgent whisper as he tried to coerce an agreement from the toughest nut in the bowl, after which the rest of us would tumble. And it was on occasions such as these that Martin, the fantasist and the man, was best revealed.

A pallid mixture of red and white body parts, Martin was on the short side and always dressed in a brown, two-piece suit, a grey V-necked jumper, white shirt and a scrawny little tie of some indeterminate mud colour; on his small feet there would be a pair of scuffed, round-toed, lace-up shoes. Where Les wore silk socks, as diaphanous as a debutante's hosiery, Martin wore grey cotton socks in which the elastic had snapped around their tops, thus lowering them in wrinkled tubes to reveal a patch of hairless flesh, the colour of cold chicken, above each ankle.

It was this last detail more than any other which seemed to shed light on the reality of Martin's character, which was that of a sulky small boy, refused permission to carry a box of matches, or ordered to wash his dirty knees. And it was this tell-tale demeanour which sat so at odds with the one activity which dominated Martin's attitudes and conversation – his membership of the Territorial Army as a lance corporal 'sapper'. I felt sorry for Martin, because it was his determination to be tough which most revealed his vulnerability. Despite the fact that he was known throughout not only Waste, but a floor up to Office Maintenance and a floor down to Reception and

Mailing, as a veteran bore of the most suffocating kind, I would always try to hear out his interminable anecdotes (in which he invariably starred as the old lag who knew the ropes, in the face of foolhardy revisionism) with an expression of slack-jawed amazement at his cunning, and gapes of incredulity at the stupidity of his detractors. Sometimes, when I'm caught on the loop of hate and self-loathing, I know that I am just like Martin.

Martin fancied the office to be a civilian version of his platoon and he would shout out things like 'Get that man to the guard room!' whenever someone made a mistake, to which his colleagues would reply, if it was someone like Roy or Luke, 'Fuck off, spotty'. Frequently short of an audience, Martin would at least find somebody to talk to by asking them a highly technical question about the Army, to which they could not possibly the know the answer – the correct way to reassemble the parts of a Bren gun, for instance. The trap sprung, he would then launch into a detailed explanation, in the forceful, slightly sarcastic tone of a sergeant major tutoring a new recruit.

He even tried this with the young women in the office, none of whom was much older than twenty, but all of whom could stare directly ahead of themselves, unblinking, while rotating a piece of chewing gum between their upper and lower teeth in a way which would shatter the confidence of a five-star general. This expression conveyed the full impact of boredom, contempt and indifference to whoever might be rash, naive or stupid enough to try to penetrate its total exclusion zone of browned-off, self-policing sisterhood.

It was well known around the office that the only thing which could rouse any of the women from this seeming stupor was their own conversation between themselves. But Martin, oblivious to such hostility, would battle on and you could hear him saying, 'But I wouldn't do that if I was you because the firing pin'll drop out', above the listless scraping of plastic spoons around the insides of empty yoghurt pots, or the idle flicking over of the thin, sticky pages of a gargantuan mail-order catalogue.

It would be much easier, I sometimes think, if you didn't have to talk to anyone at the office; if you could just take your work and your sandwiches into a little booth, and go home when you'd finished. Perhaps you already can. It isn't that the people at the office are unpleasant – or, at any rate, any more or less unpleasant than you or I can be; it is the strain of all those conversations, which, without the bonding of some shared sensibility, can become nothing more than a series of agreements, pointlessly pursued to their inevitable conclusion. Knuckles whiten on clenched fists in trouser pockets, and mouths ache from smiling, because offices sour sincerity.

The office is full of ingested feelings and that's what

makes it so unhealthy; ingested feelings are how people can get one of those illnesses that we're all afraid we might have growing inside us, from cancer to madness – the fear that we've got an alien on board. And that's what I call my fear of mortality, which is the same, I suppose, as my fear of redundancy: 'having an alien on board'.

I was probably thinking along these lines, way back then, as I was waiting in my phone box for Fat Val to pick up. To tell you the truth, even as I was picturing her phone, with its oblong patches of greying adhesive, left behind from when stickers with useful extension numbers on them had been ripped off, I was feeling sick with ingested feelings. Fat Val, I presumed, swollen with disaffection, disgust and despair, would listen to my impersonation of a loyal worker distraught at his sudden, incapacitating illness with a lengthy exhalation of anger and impatience.

I could see her, as I had seen her so often before, hunched over the phone and twisting the plume of her ratty top-knot as she heard unwelcome news with long-suffering sighs. Then again, I was challenging the might of the office in order to win the day; I couldn't shake off the beckoning mood of the morning: that urging of exploration through the City's response to the sun, a symphony of impressions, which would find its coda in the long, final chord of sunset – a day in The Life. I—

''ello, Waste.'

It was Fat Val, at last. She pronounced Waste 'wyste', in a single, half-hearted sigh. In brave but weakened tones I explained my sudden predicament: the warning tremors of nausea that had caused my stomach to buckle the previous evening, but which I had disregarded; the fact that I had felt *perfectly okay* until I got to London Bridge, but then how I had felt sick again; how perhaps it was the weather or the slow, creeping poison of a dodgy sandwich. I chattered on relentlessly, becoming aware that my enfeebled words were dropping like gravel into the black depths of an eerie well, with not the faintest answering splash. This time, I thought, I must have really pushed the limits of enough. Finally, my voice trailed away and the blackness seemed to loom up at me, out of which the beating of leathery wings would soon be heard, as Fat Val dispatched her demons. But a solitary pair of moaned syllables – 'All right . . .' ('orrite') – was all that I received. Fat Val could not have cared less; and how could I have been so arrogant as to presume otherwise? Now, twenty years later, I can understand why. For Valerie Mason, the office was malignant in its constancy; her depression built, layer on sickening layer, not through the occurrence of crises and errors, but through the sheer inevitablity of being caught in a kind of swamp of boredom and irritation: a common enough complaint, but translated through some quirk in Val's chemistry into a permanent condition which weighed her down, physically, and which made every movement an effort. And I know that I am often just like Val as well.

Did Les the virtuoso have an eye on Val's job, waiting for the day when she would take extended sick leave for good? This had been rumoured but somehow I doubted it; Les's distinction was his panache, the controlled performance of the figure skater, saluting his ovation beneath the circling, multicoloured starlight of a glitter-ball. Command was not his thing but specialization; Martin, on the other hand, given half a chance would have issued us all with ranks and numbers before finally shooting himself in a bunker.

But I left all of this behind me as I swung the heavy door of the telephone box back open and walked into the brilliant sunshine which was waiting for me at the end of the alley. It was like slipping into a warm bath. The knots of tension just beneath the nape of my neck appeared to loosen and dissolve; I undid the top button of my shirt, pulled off my tie and stuffed it into my pocket.

My route lay west: up Lambeth Hill and Friday Street towards Saint Paul's, and on with the slowness of afternoon, to walk towards the setting sun, down Ludgate Hill and up through Holborn, by way of back streets and courtyards, following the hot, white dust of building sites and the cool cloisters of shadow which edged the highest buildings. No Venetian maze of alleys and bridges, I thought, would be as romantic as this journey of the solitary walker through the ancient centre of London. And no tourist's eyes would gaze across the lagoon at dusk with a contentment equal to mine when I reached the Thames once more that evening. For by then, I believed, I would own the romance of my route. But, do you know, I walked all day and nothing happened? Or, rather, something worse than nothing happened: because I lost that glimpse of the extraordinary, and that moment of certainty which I had experienced on London Bridge, within half an hour of setting out on my search to witness its source. I was shut out from the cafés and the crowds, the grey bustle in the entrances of the tube stations, and the quickening currents of the lunch hour. I felt a stale dullness where I had anticipated magic; as though, away from the taut restraints of the office routine, the day had become formless, the mainstring of its mechanism slackened, rather than strengthened, by my stolen freedom. And there was my lesson.

And this is what I meant to say about that terrible feeling of redundancy, of having nowhere to go and no place: those rare experiences of transcendence which the city can offer as sacred gifts are never given lightly; it is all one process of effort and reward, or work and pay, which grants the unexpected vision in the midst of the daily round, and makes you feel, if only for a second, that you can see beyond the seen amongst the limitless streets and faces to a place that you can call your own. All romantics, perhaps, are pornographers at heart — arousing themselves with a subtle detail, the promise of which could never be kept.

TWO

The crowded morning commuter train, having jolted and rattled the last half mile between Clapham Junction and Victoria Station, came to a slow, lethargic halt on the barren span of Grosvenor Bridge, a bridge built only for commuter trains. The neighbouring elegance of Chelsea Bridge, this morning, was nothing more than a grey outline, seen through a pale mist the colour of violets. Just behind us, the gutted remains of Battersea Power Station looked like an abandoned hulk, beached beyond an arid delta of tracks and points. The four great chimneys were higher than the mist and touched at their tops by sunshine. To one side of them, the derelict cranes looked as fragile as the skeletons of insects.

I feel sure that I have a memory of the old coal barges, moored beneath the winching gear, and of watching the silvery coal being carried away on a steep conveyor belt. There is a melancholy which is particular to empty places which used to be busy: a sense of lives disdained by time.

Because it was cold when we set off from the suburbs – it is only April, after all – the windows of the carriages were streaming with condensation. Here and there, bored passengers had wiped a space with their palm or sleeve to peer out through. Even as they stared down at the bleached cinders, or gazed into the mist, you could feel how the stillness outside had found its way into the carriage. The rustle of a newspaper, a short cough, the sudden snapping open of the locks on a briefcase: all of these sounds were amplified in the silence of our apathy, resignation or impatience. Our huddle of humanity, our mass of scarves and overcoats, polished shoes, handbags, gloves and hangovers, could only defend its dignity by learning how to wait. Another train pulled up beside us, our mirror.

South of the river, beyond the cosy comfort of gentrified Dulwich or Wimbledon, far from the warming glow of London proper, there exists that furthest rim of suburbia from which our train sets out each morning. To anyone used to the speed and spontaneity of urban life, our far-flung suburbs with their libraries and recreation grounds, tandoori restaurants and civic offices would seem like nothing less than an aerial photograph of mortality. If the city is a machine for living, then some people would think of our suburbs as a machine for dying.

But there we all were again, this morning, on the 07.57 – running eight minutes late. We were from beyond the city walls – yokels come to Athens – with the damp of the park on our clothes and hair: the smell of fine rain. And once you boil down the fat turkey of a platitude, you're usually left with an extremely complicated pile of bones. And I was thinking of how we all tend to see the world as divided between Us and Them. It's always like that in the office, anyway: Us and Them; and They are always being unjust to Us. That's what we tell each other, to get by.

The office begins with commuting. I once saw some pictures of those trains in Japan which are fitted out like miniature offices so that the workers can put in an extra half hour almost as soon as the morning *miso* has gone down. You dishonour the firm by falling asleep. But as I looked around my train, this morning, it was pretty much business as usual. There was a young man to my right who was copy-editing a neighbourhood newsletter. He was wearing a pale brown overcoat, tightly belted, and he kept looking out of the window as he roamed around in his thoughts. His eyes were almost as pale as his skin and he had a beard that just wasn't coming together. He looked as though he had no social skills, but was passionately enthusiastic about one subject – which could have been anything from white water rafting to modern ballet. The thing is, you never know; and this is fundamental to office life.

So often I have been surprised by sudden disclosures about the personal interests of people in the office – leaving aside the rumours about their sex lives. 'Graham does a lot for the World Wildlife Fund.' Or 'Wendy goes in for country dancing.' To me, the difficulty lies in the fact that I have yet to develop a language which enables me to discuss life beyond the office in the office. Friendship should be the oil which keeps the mechanism of office life running smoothly; but there always seemed to be some grit in the works, some erratic fragment of behaviour or information which finds its way into the best natured of offices, and begins to raise the temperature. The office keeps an unsteady course between formality and a kind of tainted domesticity – one big dysfunctional family. And of course, the twentieth century has been dominated by the conflict between the individual and the organization. It's all Us and Them.

These days, individualism itself (Us) is packaged by the organization (Them) and sold along with starter homes and coffee grinders and everything else. I once read a copy of *Oz* magazine; a teenager from Reading got it right, back in 1970: 'The media's tactic is "take it over, package it, sell it back to itself." We haven't infiltrated them, they've infiltrated us. Now the revolution is a groovy way to sell things.'

A lot of people these days don't seem to be conscious of the fact – or don't really care – that the organization is even selling them the lifestyle which they think is challenging the organization. The organization's got them taped; it's very clever – expert in the voodoo arts of marketing, packaging and advertising. Commodifying individualism is the organization's simple way of dealing with the perversity of human nature. If you want to sell a car, package the idea of protest.

This morning, a woman was sitting opposite me on the train, reading *The Mayor of Casterbridge* with her chin pushed down into a bright scarlet muffler. Her book mark advertised a chain of hotels which also runs ferries to Holland. She had wrapped her overcoat around herself as closely as possible, and every time the man sitting next to her turned the pages of his newspaper she let out a short, angry sigh and flinched. She looked like one of those people who can't make a journey on public transport of any length without reporting later that somebody's bag was digging into her leg. But I could understand her territorial hostility towards the man beside her, whose florid jowls began to bulge over his pale blue shirt collar when he reached the bottom of the page. His eyes were alert and his expression, it seemed, was reflecting what he thought the news was worth: 'Is the news up to scratch? I'm a fair man, but busy, and I've no time to waste on sub-standard news.' Already, he had judged and found guilty a half-page story about the proposed redevelopment of the arts venues on the South Bank, headlined 'Time To Get Rid Of These Eyesores'.

Over the years, wandering to and from the office, I have seen whole districts of London torn open by urban planners in the name of creating a cosmopolitan Utopia. I call this process Death By Cappuccino, and I date its maturity from the regeneration of Covent Garden in the early 1980s. One day, the whole of London will be a single, twenty-four-hour shop, with a coffee bar in it the size of Pimlico. The search is on, I often think, for the Lowest Common Denominator of Everything; and perhaps that lowest common denominator will be some kind of superstore: the Ultimate Mothership.

What I liked about the brutalism of the old South Bank was its indifference to being liked or loathed; under a winter sky, the colour of a week old bruise, those slab façades of weathered concrete had an air of gravitas: they looked grown up. And the pillared spaces beneath them, like hidden grottoes filled with grey light on spring evenings, or the overground bunkers of the concert halls and gallery, reflecting the mottled sky in their long, high windows – they seemed to respect the need for meditation and enquiry. Topped by the silently alternating colours of Philip Vaughan's sculpture in neon, here was a place where ideas were never meant to be replaced by image, an uncomfortable place, even.

Years ago, on winter nights, I would make my way back to Waterloo Station through the deserted, softly-lit precincts which connected the angular buildings of the South Bank. These precincts converged on a raised walkway, which ran behind the full length of the Royal Festival Hall, and faced the hundreds of identically square windows of the old Shell Building. Wealds of ice, black in the gleam of artificial light, would crack beneath my shoes as I walked along; from time to time an icy wind would pick up, funnelled between the buildings into a ragged blade of cold which cut right through my old raincoat and made me lower my head as I pushed forward. And then the wind would drop again, and I could hear my footsteps in the still, frosty air, as though there was no other sound in the world.

Sometimes, I would be making my way home from a concert on the other side of the river. In those days I had a friend called Paul, and he would have trudged off to Embankment or Temple stations – his way lay east, to Upton Park. And these memories remind me that the whole business of commuting can be seen as a repeated journey between the warm, infantilist innocence of the suburbs, and the heady, volatile experience of the city. It was almost as though I could roam about the vast labyrinth of London's streets, searching for something, so long as I was tethered to the safety of the suburbs. But then, first weekly and then daily, and then more or less hourly, I would find myself thinking. 'What happens if you can never get home again?' And I saw myself, a wraith on Aldwych or Chancery Lane, doomed to walk forever, gripping the collars of my coat in one puny fist as I endlessly circled Holborn, Museum Street and the shabby, freezing Bloomsbury squares. I saw a premonition in monochrome in which the little paths across Gordon, Montague and Russell Squares were hidden by drifts of dead leaves, through which I was wading at the onset of winter. There would be no more trains home: the departure boards of all the great south London stations would be mercilessly blank for all eternity . . .

There was a sudden jolt, and the rising, shuddering drone of the train's engine coming back to life was followed by the male exhalation of its air-brakes; a jolt more, and we were off again, slipping out of the thinning, violet-coloured mist – which was now being burned away by the sun – and clattering over the last few sets of points which lead through what is known, in technical slang, as the throat of Victoria Station.

You could feel the air relax in the carriage, followed almost immediately by the passengers preparing to gather themselves together, in the collective 'here we go again' which also, most probably, kicks off each new phase of reincarnation. Soon we were all grouped – restless, patient, aloof or pig-headed – in a shapeless queue towards the sliding doors of our carriage. I was looking at the back and shoulders of a man with greying brown hair who was wearing a beige raincoat; his palm was pressed against the rubber pad, which, once the 'Doors Open' panel was illuminated, would release us all to our destinies. The train crawled forward to its final halt, and the back of the man's hand flexed in readiness.

Arriving at one of London's main stations during the rush hour, you become aware of looking at the backs of people's heads as you all troop off towards the concourse; you catch a glimpse, maybe, of steam drifting away from the cooling ducts on a roof high above you. You pass the perspex window of the platform controller's booth and see the imprint of someone's fist, with cracks spreading out from the central dent like the strands of a cobweb.

Some days, the city appears to be heaving itself to work in a surly temper, with queues, delays and muttered oaths. On days like that, your progress can no more be hurried than if you were in the sleepiest country town; patience, above all, and detachment, are required if you are going to reach the office without being led off the autobahn of benign routine and sucked into the gridlock of impotent rage.

Since I started working at North Row, I have been using Victoria Station every day. For some reason, this felt like a demotion from the modern muscularity of London Bridge. To me, Victoria Station has the air of the West End: a commercial thoroughfare, down-at-heel but lively with shops and kiosks. In the minuscule cabin of a Bureau de Change, two small Filipino women were wearing rosettes which proclaimed 'Make A Friend Of Jesus'. The boy serving customers from The Bagel Factory looked like a young academic, press-ganged into wearing a straw hat. In Knickerbox and The Sock Shop, women were putting garments on hangers as the torrent of commuters thundered passed their open doors.

In order to avoid this quickening current of workers, hurrying towards the underground station, I usually make a detour around the back of the newsagent's which effectively separates the station into two halves:

Platforms 2 to 8, and Platforms 9 to 18. Each side has a different personality, a tone of character too subtle to define, but undeniably apparent. I have never found Platform 1. Someone at the office told me that it leads directly to the Houses of Parliament, so that in the event of a nuclear attack – such as we were always fearing in the Sixties – the Members of Parliament could be whizzed off to an underground shelter before the capital was vaporized in a single horizontal sheet of white light.

Every day, I tell myself that I am taking this evasive action of walking around the back of the newsagent's, rather than being carried along by the main throng of the commuters, in order to prove that I am not bound to the daily grind. But why should I try to pretend this to myself? The daily grind is a benign routine, when it is held in place by the right dynamic of effort and reward, and it can offer you a constancy and a place in the world which is as certain as the North Star. And yet we all claim to hate the common herd.

This morning, like every morning, I stopped to have a cup of coffee at the little café on the station. This café – one of a big chain – is staffed by friendly Algerians who are kung fu enthusiasts. I have seen them practising their head kicks on the sacks of unroasted Blue Mountain beans. There is usually a copy of *The Tao of Bruce Lee* on their staff table, between the heaped ashtray and a few loose pages of the morning paper. They always ask 'How are you?' as they knock the compacted dregs out of the espresso filter. There is Ricky, Mustafa, Bruce and some guy who looks like a computer-generated portrait of a Messiah. Because they don't know me, they like me, and agree with everything I say.

Today, I took my cup of coffee and sat down at one of the little aluminium tables which are grouped around the glass-fronted entrance to the café. You could see the sunshine streaming down through the high canopy over the platforms; it reminded me of the light pouring into a cathedral, and it made me want to be leaving on a long journey.

Facing Platforms 8 to 2, I could watch the last of the commuter trains arriving with their human cargo, and the first of the off-peak morning trains, virtually empty but still rich with the smell of their disgorged load, sliding out again to stations which would be equally empty. The strange, violet-coloured mist would have lifted, and, away from the office, there would be the waiting threat of an empty day as well.

Now that I'm working in the West End, at an office which is known merely as North Row, I can either take the underground to Green Park and walk or take two underground trains to Bond Street and walk a shorter distance. But in the mornings, the air of expense and exclusivity which hangs around Green Park and the walk to North Row through Berkeley Square makes me feel slightly sick.

At that time of day, when you tend to feel so

vulnerable, I find it hard to walk past the shops and showrooms of the luxury district which are selling sports cars, Sumerian artefacts and gold-plated hairbrushes. The idea of such extravagance makes me feel light-headed and clammy, like the thought of drinking brandy before breakfast. I will only have got half way to the office and a great weariness seems to seep through my body, settling like sediment on the dark bed of my thoughts.

What it boils down to is this: that I suddenly feel as though I am personally responsible for the constant maintenance of a cripplingly extravagant and wasteful lifestyle; or, looking up at the windows of the suites in The Ritz, that the sheer effort of so much luxury somehow devolves on to my own undefended shoulders – which have yet to gather their day's strength. This is a symptom of some fundamental unease, the precise nature of which I have decided to uncover.

In the meantime, I find that I need to enter my day through the back door, as it were, of the short walk up the south side of Oxford Street from Bond Street station, to the turning down Lumley Street which leads to North Row.

But this morning, as I was sitting outside the café on Victoria Station, watching the morning trains, a young woman – in her middle twenties, at a guess – came and sat down at a neighbouring table. She was one of those women whom you see sometimes – but very rarely – during the working day, and with whom, across the vast chasm which separates you as

44

strangers, you dream for an instant of commencing a grand love affair.

This woman, to me anyway, could have passed for the young Claudia Cardinale. There was something about her grey eyes, pale skin and delicate hands which was immediately restful: an openness in her expression of unimpeachable honesty, generous to the world and trusting in a fundamental decency. Everything about her, from her auburn hair in its French pleat, to the languid manner in which she crossed her legs (she was wearing a charcoal-coloured trouser suit, with some kind of roll-neck jumper) seemed to smile at the world from a distance.

Adolescence for her must have been a country easily conquered, from which she had no need to banish awkwardness or doubt; there would have been no resistance to the force of her nature, which was driven by this same smiling openness to all that life might have to offer, and which was made eloquent in the way she dried her hair, or leaned to one side to fasten an earring, or listened, unblinking, to whatever words might pit themselves against her self-possession.

I was so wrapped up in these imaginings of hope and fresh beginnings that I thought the woman had turned to smile at me; I smiled back, feeling the creases around my eyes, and hoping to answer the warmth and welcome of her glance with a look of friendliness and understanding. But the man at whom she was actually smiling was standing directly behind me. I gave a little jump of surprise when I realized that he was so near and knocked against the table, spilling my coffee. The young woman, of course, noticed none of this, and seemed to be drawing the man towards her with her smiling eyes. When I turned and looked at the man, I couldn't blame her. He was maybe in his late forties; his neatly cut hair was silver, his handsome profile was lean, and his eyes, too, were that shade of grey which deepens the black of the pupils. He was dressed in a dark blue suit, with a pale blue shirt and a navy blue, square-ended, knitted tie. He had one of those expensive raincoats, the colour of dry cement, which looks even more expensive when it is heavily creased.

Here, to be sure, was the urbane, wealthy, older man, whose very weariness is somehow erotic, and whose highly developed taste for beauty has led him to discard an entire harem of sophisticated women — habituées of *la vie deluxe*, born to bask on borrowed yachts — in order to snatch a few minutes at a concourse café with this young woman, whose eyes matched his and whose sincerity promised to turn life into a miraculous adventure. In fact, he was her father.

The young woman's accent, I heard, had that particular jaunty twang which you can always hear around the shops and offices of London: it's a declamatory tone of voice, in which the speakers usually tend to be commentating on their own conversation. I suddenly thought of people in their offices around Regent Street and Hanover Square, sitting behind their cluttered desks, as they made extremely long phone calls. The young woman remained, to my furtive glances, as beautiful as before; but the equation of assessment had kicked into place, which makes you consider a person's affectations in retaliation for the impossibility of knowing them. This is a despicable trait, symptomatic of one's own insecurities. But there you go.

As I walked away from the café, towards the entrance of Victoria underground station, I remembered how Paul had talked about reaching a stage where he saw nothing but his own affectations, or what he believed to be affectations. He had hit a state of permanent self-consciousness; unable to get off the gyratory of self-loathing, he became an alcoholic. The world had become unbearable for him, with no relief save drunkenness: ambition was pointless, culture a joke and love an impossibility. In time, without the anaesthetic of alcohol, he found himself unequal to the impact of living. He disappeared for three days and was found unconscious beneath a cashpoint machine in Cricklewood; when he was roused, he withdrew a hundred pounds and then collapsed again.

Six months after he got out of hospital, I met Paul for a cup of coffee in a big counter service Italian restaurant on Charlotte Street. It was a winter's afternoon, a Sunday, and intensely cold. The light in the street was as grey

as the pavement. Everywhere was held in that quiet
which heralds the first flakes of snow, drifting between
the buildings with a silent urgency. The restaurant, as
spacious and gloomy as any canteen, and smelling of fried
food, was furnished in the Tyrolean style, with green
wooden chairs and brightly painted frescoes depicting
the Italian lakes. There was nobody else at any of the
tables; a middle-aged Italian woman, with black hair and
a sullen expression, was sitting behind the cash register
at the end of the counter.

Paul had arrived before me. An accountant by pro-
fession, he had easily found a new job; his previous
employers had paid for him to dry out in a private clinic
and then sacked him. But that's American banks for you;
where I was working – this must have been in the early
Nineties – you'd have been lucky to get the afternoon
off. I had been expecting the usual idea of the reformed
alcoholic, a fragile figure who moved as though he were
made of glass; but Paul looked exactly the same as he
always had, only his skin was clearer and he'd put on
a bit of weight – chocolate, he told me. The last time
I had seen him – or, rather, the last I had seen of him
– was his back, as he pushed open the heavy door of a
crowded pub in Holborn.

Back then, standing behind him, the heat and the noise
as he had opened the pub's door had all but knocked me
down; I had tugged the sleeve of his raincoat to say that I
didn't see the point of going inside, but he either didn't

hear me or didn't want to hear. He disappeared into the press of the crowd, which seemed to yield to his slight pressure and then suck him in, before closing around him and taking him from my sight. But he'd been more or less incoherent by that time, anyway, and I hadn't been sad to see him go.

Now he was sitting before me in the empty restaurant, more embarrassed than anything; he was smoking one cigarette after another, and he drank his scalding coffee in two long mouthfuls, as though his throat was made of cast iron. I asked him about his new job and where he was living, but he didn't have much to say about either. He said he spent hours on an exercise bike, reciting the Lord's Prayer. Fairly soon our conversation had become like a long, dull street, all the turnings off which turn out to be cul-de-sacs. I realize, now, that I had wanted him to offer me some sentimental parable.

Today, thinking back to that Sunday afternoon as I hurried down the dirty steps into the underground, it occurred to me that life itself had closed around Paul and sucked him under, with a far greater malignancy than any pub ever had. I had first met Paul when we were teenagers; he smoked Sobranie Black Russian cigarettes and always had his nose in a book. But even the suburb where we both lived − a maze of quiet roads and colourless parades of shops, spreading out around two dual carriageways and a railway line − appeared to trap him under the immensity of its open sky.

The City claimed him as soon as he left university and within it he saw the triumph of stupidity. He should have been a Burroughs or a Rimbaud – but he thought that they were stupid as well; the black heart of his nihilism admitted no allegiance to any cultural icons. He was an aesthete who could see only the enemies of beauty; he burned out his sudden enthusiasms. Johnny Rotten reminded him of Old Man Steptoe.

I set Paul up, high on a pedestal, as a Hero Of Our Times. He reminded me of a beautiful woman who tries her best to be ugly – but I was too naive, or too stupid, to stop and consider why that should be. But Paul has lingered as my intellectual conscience, on and off, even though I haven't seen him in the best part of a decade.

The office at North Row is a red brick, five-storey block which was built in the early 1950s as relief accommodation for a division of the Home Civil Service. Our lot took it over in the late Sixties and, despite many changes, the premises themselves have retained an indelible, indestructible air of austere, institutional officialdom. This is a building designed for tea trolleys, flattened vowels and snoods.

But there have been significant changes.

You used to go into the building through a pair of double swing-doors which had thick panes of glass set into their metal frames. A lift faced you – as it does today – and a staircase flanked the lift. To the left and right of the lobby, which was always obscured by a kind of twilight, dark corridors led off to the Post Room, on one side – which was noisy, masculine and Spartan – and to the Office Registry on the other – which was quiet, feminine, and as orderly as a hospital ward.

The Post Room was run by Old Tom, a short-tempered, elderly man who inspired the respect of the heavily built boys who worked for him by treating all the other employees in the office as though they were morons. Old Tom played the part of a martyr to procedure: a man whose life had been ruined by everybody else's inability to fill in the Post Room paperwork correctly.

People in the office are often described, and known, by their first name and a prefatory adjective; Old Tom's favourite was Young Tom – a baby-faced, asexual school leaver who was always wide-eyed with admiration at the strong-arm tactics of his peers in the Post Room. He enjoyed the protection of Old Tom and would flit about the more exclusive areas of the building with the swagger of a bureaucratic Puck.

As the dank caverns of the Post Room smelt of sweat, cardboard and cigarette smoke, so the evenly-lit rooms of the Office Registry smelt of furniture polish, photocopying paper and a compound of scents which began with hand-cream and ended with Alpine Fern air-freshener. Men were often nervous about going into the Office Registry, because it usually seemed as though the women who worked in there were engaged in some sacred feminine ritual involving personal hygiene and photographs of babies.

The Office Registry (OR) was run by a kindly, quietly spoken woman from Beckenham called Yvonne. She was one of those people who is always smiling, even when they are complaining; she looked as though she had been designed in the 1960s, complete with headscarf and shopping bag, and she always had a friendly word for everyone. Her staff were for the most part young married women; one of them — I can't remember her name — would dress up as an elf every Christmas and push her Internal Mail trolley around the building decked out in a little red tunic and a pointed hat with a bell on it. For the rest of the year, however, she could silence a room with a glance.

But these descriptions of North Row, and of the opposed masculinity and femininity of the Post Room and Office Registry, can only be written in the past tense. That particular universe — and the office becomes the universe for the people who work there — reached critical mass in the late 1980s. At that point, a powerful coalition between the Management Services Department, Staff Accommodation and the Internal Audit, decreed that North Row must modernize and get hip to the ethos of private sector professionalism which had seeped out of the City to inflame the ambitions of nearly every office and institution, be it ever so humble or grand, the length and breadth of Britain. To this end, the Management Services Department (or Management Services Group, as they started to call themselves) called in the expertise and general panache of an independent corporate identity consultancy: Arvonn Wysemann.

For three months, North Row lay as inert as a drugged patient and was probed and prodded by a cluster of smooth-looking individuals with clipboards, who were described by anyone in charge as the corporate identity team — CIT. Mr Fallowfield, a florid alcoholic who worked in his own humid office on the fourth floor, and who was turned on by any intimation of authority, went so far as to describe the CIT as a hit squad. He rather tried to attach himself to them, in fact, and you could see the consultants using every trick in the training course to try and get him fired. But to no avail. What the Territorial Army had been to Martin in Waste, so Arvonn Wysemann became to 'Shakey' Fallowfield. To any one who would listen, he would list the consultancy's many skills: ratifying, problem solving, behavioural psychology, industrial ergonomics . . .

The first result of Arvonn Wysemann's extensive review of North Row's function, image, ergonomics and environmental presentation was that every square inch of floorspace was covered in grey carpeting. As a consequence of this, an acre or so of varnished parquet flooring disappeared.

These grey carpets, however, turned out to be the

ambassadors of a far more sinister intention. As they spread throughout the building from the lobby, so each area that they touched was drastically revised. The first victims were Yvonne's Office Registry and Old Tom's Post Room: a fully computerized data and dispatch system made anachronisms of both these institutions. It was only a matter of weeks before the whole of the ground floor and its personnel bore little resemblance to what and who had been there before. Early retirements and staff relocations flourished like spring daffodils in Hyde Park.

The carpets swept onwards and upwards, leaving in their wake an office upheaval the like of which had never been seen before. Ancient enclosures and venerable cubby holes were ripped open and exposed to the brutal light of the New Professionalism, prior to their destruction. It was rather like gassing badgers. Strange characters who had been peaceably plodding about their office routines for the best part of twenty years were suddenly the targets for the passing around of brown circulation envelopes – the donations into which their colleagues would pay for their leaving presents. And wherever the grey carpet worked its revisionist influence, a framed print was hung on the wall to mark its passing.

Thus, masterpieces of modern art came to represent the triumph of the new order. Where once Old Tom and his boys had lounged or cursed beneath a few cork noticeboards and a goodwill wet T-shirt calendar from some printing rep, now details of Monet's water lilies or Cezanne's bathers took their place above the screens and keyboards of a half dozen workstations. Yvonne's kittens-in-a-basket disappeared for good, their pert playfulness exchanged for the shadowy limbs of a Degas ballerina.

A certain historical thematizing conducted the passage of these framed prints, upwards through the building. Sickert, Whistler, Roger Fry and Duncan Grant on the first floor; Hepworth, Moore and Elizabeth Frink on the second, and so on. By the time that they got to 'Shakey' Fallowfield, trembling in a haze of Scotch on four, his volatile expansiveness was all but mirrored by the chunks of abstract expressionism which marked his removal.

Prints and carpets, therefore, defined the manner in which Arvonn Wysemann plucked North Row from the artery-clogging apathy of Austerity Britain and put it on the high fibre diet of Eighties professionalism. And what the ethos of this professionalism appeared to boil down to was the denial of the individual's right to fail. Once those prints were up, everything and everyone was accountable to a strict procedure of assessment; and at the heart of this procedure, as determined by its inventors, lay a masculine fetish for communication skills and information technology. This was the era of the boot camp training course, where you all had to pretend to be different parts of an engine, like some weird piece of communist theatre from the 1930s.

This was also the time which marked a discovery about myself, that I jinxed technology as surely as if I was ripping out the plugs. Computers crashed, software went haywire, and sophisticated electronic mailing systems began whizzing messages off to who knows where in the chilly straits of cyberspace the moment I so much as looked at a mouse mat. I would sit before the dead-eyed screen of my terminal with an air of baffled innocence, as stocky men with pagers clipped to their belts, wearing the expressions of exasperated zoo-keepers trying to corner an escaped rhino, slipped successions of trouble-shooting discs into my stack. They would then look on in complete disbelief as my system remained stubbornly down.

Through this I gained something of an occult reputation throughout the building, and there were some people who were genuinely scared by my malign influence on their precious technology. IT, after all, was the single hook upon which the office had hung nearly all of its hopes. Despite this, they kept me on.

The old refrigerated vending machine was replaced by a group of smart young women who arrived at the office in the middle of the morning carrying baskets filled with esoteric baguettes and low fat yoghurt. Men and women who had occupied their positions in upper-middle and upper management with a certain degree of donnish cynicism were suddenly straining to appear dynamic and ravenous for results. They would haul themselves into breakfast meetings and spoke in a strange new language of acronyms and initials – 'FUG', 'TUK' and 'HURL' were my favourites – with a Maoist urgency to be seen as orthodox.

Not that I retained, or retain, any nostalgia or sentimentality for Old Tom, Yvonne or the vending machine: that former office which had been buried like the dust of a Roman town beneath the swathes of grey carpet.

If tomorrow belongs to anyone, they can keep it.

THREE

Unequal, as usual, to the opulence of Green Park, I travelled on the Jubilee Line to Bond Street station. However hard I try, this is a bad time of day for me. The tasks ahead seem like so many bones in a mouthful of fish. Then, everything appears formless, pointless but faintly threatening. When I try to put my finger on it, it's like trying to remember a nightmare.

This morning, I saw my inverted reflection in the black mirrors which flank the escalator rail in the West One centre. This happens every day, and every day I recall a line in some film: 'Let us all reflect.' The phrase pops into my head like a blocking signal. Another phrase which occurs like that is 'Magic moments' – from the Perry Como song.

But once, in one of those West End pubs where the carpets are blackened and sticky with spilt beer and there's never anywhere to sit, I found myself watching an uneasy couple who were squeezed behind a small table to one side of a cigarette machine. Around them, noisy circles of drinkers were increasing their unease.

This couple might have been on a first date, a blind

date or a last date; the man looked as though he ought to be something important in the Berlin Philharmonic: he was young, but his closely-cropped hair was already turning grey and his refined features were sharpened by the spider-thin glasses which he wore halfway down his nose. He had a skier's tan, and his appearance and bearing made you think of a modern, European school of efficiency and affluence. He was dressed in a black suit, with a pale blue shirt and a gold tie. That much I could see beneath the short black coat – cashmere, at a glance – which he had not found the room to take off.

Whenever I think of him I imagine a life which I envy: a life in perfect order, planned as a sequence of efforts and rewards which would ultimately lead to the ultimate reward of healthy and happy autonomy – cycling holidays in Bavaria, just you, her and the lap-top. Or I imagined him buying an off-road Land Cruiser and one of those torches that are used by the American police. But at the time I actually saw him, he looked extremely unhappy.

The woman sitting opposite him, who had to keep jerking her low bar stool even further under the table as the crowds in the pub began to grow louder and noisier, was perhaps feeling more awkward than unhappy. She was tall, with long, brown hair which fell in heavy ringlets between her shoulder blades; her face was pale and oval-shaped, which set off the deep crimson of her lipstick and the darkness of her big eyes. Her eyebrows were exquisitely thinned and shaped into two angled lines, which gave her a serious expression. But she was simply looking down at the table, to a point just beyond her gin and tonic. The gin and tonic looked tepid and watery, its glass running with condensation.

Attempting to lean forward the young man seemed as though he was trying to find the right thing to say that would calm a volatile situation. From where I was watching you could see that every fibre of his being was concentrated on drawing the woman back to him – or her attention, at any rate – from the place behind the sea wall of her silence. The woman, still staring down at the table, not blinking, was rubbing the nape of her neck with the ends of her long fingers in a swift, nervous gesture. Her eyes were quite rounded as she did this, and her hypnotized gaze reminded me of that moment when you put your cold hands into a basin of warm water and become momentarily stupefied.

But then her companion took a quick breath and said 'Let us all reflect'; and she looked up at him with a frown, but continued to rub her neck. The ice cap of the moment was beginning to crack, but having got this far the young man seemed to lose courage. I just made out the words 'not necessarily' and 'quiet' before the woman, too, began to thaw. The man's accent had turned out to be more Hounslow than Hamburg, and she had that same south London twang. After this, they became quite lively; she put her fingers up to her mouth and laughed in a way that suggested her pleasure at having heard someone else say something that she had always wanted to say.

I don't know what it says about me that I had found myself so interested in them; or that I had been quite amazed when I heard him say 'Let us all reflect'. Boredom and loneliness perhaps? A reflex to envy the couples I see? But I've had a few girlfriends over the years. I even lived with someone for a while. It just never seemed to work out. I'd become withdrawn, the women seemed to cry a lot, or get bored, and together we'd wind up trailing around the shops. But you carry on hoping, and watching other people. 'The soul sees nothing that does not distress it on reflection', wrote Pascal cheerfully. And certainly that young man crammed between the wall, the cigarette machine and a woman's targeted silence had seemed distressed. I had felt like throwing him a paper dart, with 'Are you into Fellini?' scrawled on it. But the pub was so dark and cramped and full of smoke and people that I left soon after and walked the length of Mortimer Street in the bitter cold.

In my time I have been a dandy, a kitchen boy, a glorified filing clerk and an unacknowledged ideologue. When I've had too much to drink, I refer to myself as 'the psychic lightning conductor'. I attract karma. I even attracted karma during the interview for my current job, with Mike Bailey and Fiona Witherspoon. When they asked me whether there were any questions that I wanted to ask them, I felt a kind of energy surge

— just as Mike was tapping the blank sheet of notepaper in front of him with his biro. Because none of us was telling the truth about our situation (the job was crap and they knew it, and I didn't want to do it but needed the money) we were all being responsible for the psychic leakage which is always the consequence of dishonesty.

The chairs in the interview room had orange cushions and scratched wooden frames. There was a spider plant standing in a dusty saucer on the window-sill. Behind Mike and Fiona, written in red felt-tip pen on an oblong white board, were the words 'agenda-setting' and 'deskjet'. During the last few years, just as I entered the lobby of middle age, I have been troubled by the sensation, when I least expect it, of seeming to be apart from my body. During the interview I suddenly felt as though I was tethered to the here and now by nothing more than a spittle-thin line of concentration; that I was simply floating, on a kind of space walk, somewhere near the ceiling.

We were all nodding and smiling and frowning, doing that office thing of being seen to communicate. I appear to have a highly developed sense of empathy, and this distracts me from getting on, just like boredom or anger or daydreams can distract you. I think that I only got the job at North Row because I was the oldest candidate, and they'd just appointed a load of really young people to all of the neighbouring positions.

*   *   *

This morning, as I cut through the narrow streets on the south side of Oxford Street, passed the gallery of naive art and the Greek Orthodox church, passed the telephone boxes with their mosaics of adverts for prostitutes, passed the Victorian mansion flats of red brick, and the old art deco garage, I suddenly realized that the day felt more than usually acute. You know how they used to have those cards with 'Today Is The First Day Of The Rest Of Your Life' written on them? Well, it suddenly felt like that; only I had to get through something, or beyond something, in order to believe that I was going to get that new first day. It was like fumbling for the light switch in a dark room.

I had been thinking about the couple whom I had watched in that pub, and about all the couples and all the noisy circles of drinkers in all the pubs in central London; and I had the presumption to believe that I knew their lives, but not my own. I felt as though I could see, as I was making my way to the office, a wet shower curtain, heavy and limp, left hastily pulled halfway across the shower by its owner this morning; and the crumbs of toast on the kitchen table, and the digital clock on the video recorder, with its green lights enfeebled by the morning sunshine that was filling the rooms of the flat in Streatham or Lewisham or Boreham Wood.

Imagining people's empty homes while they are at the office led me to imagine the lives of strangers: all of the couples, all of the co-workers. It always begins with a detail – the lights on the video recorder, the limp, heavy shower curtain – and then spreads outwards: the mountain bike in the hall, the plates in the sink, the silence that has replaced conversation and laughter, the dog-eared books on the shelf and the cutlery in the drawer. It's a sexual thing, as well, to imagine those flats and houses.

As I walked to North Row, in the West End of London, I found myself thinking of deserted starter homes in Wimbledon or Waltham Cross; I could imagine the lingering scents of deodorant and body spray; I could hear the click of the time-switch and the dulled thump of the heating coming on. This is the molecular chain of daily events, each one triggering the next, which makes a routine for our safety. Just before midnight, I see the last trains glide noiselessly out of the deserted terminal, as though I was watching them through sound-proofed glass. I watch their red lights disappear into the darkness.

Throughout the 1980s and on into the early Nineties, my intellectual pin-up was Titus Petronius Arbiter. This was the Emperor Nero's 'arbiter of elegance', or style counsellor, whose dandyism concealed the lucidity with which he could anatomize the morals and manners of his times. Denounced to Nero as a traitor by a jealous rival within the Emperor's inner court of literary minded favourites, Petronius took his own life at his leisure, opening his veins and rebandaging them as the fancy took him, surrounded by friends, fine food and flowers, while making a list of Nero's iniquities.

In his erotic, realist portrait of his times, *The Satyricon*, Petronius gave a timeless account of the patrician classes. Talk about Us and Them. His description of the dinner party held by the millionaire and self-styled poet, Trimalchio, is particularly astute; it reminds you of all the self-obsessed micro-celebrities you see gurning out at you from the newstands every day, pushing their crap careers in the not remotely entertainment business.

And so every day I would read Petronius on the train, pushing him forward, as it were, as my champion. But now – this morning to be precise – I found myself wincing at the thought of this enthusiasm. I think that perhaps people like Petronius see the world a little bit too clearly, and that this, despite their brilliance, robs them of something vital. I was going to say, robs them of their humility – but that's not it.

There are two ways of seeing the world too clearly. The first, as endured by Petronius and my friend Paul is to grow to see only corruption, stupidity, grandiosity and cruelty wherever you look. But the destination of such an outlook will always be despair: an all-encompassing hatred of the world which is reflecting your own self-hatred. Imagine the dandy worn out by his own ennui, or the nicotine addict who ends up regarding his blackened lungs as mirrors of his troubled conscience.

But then there is a second way of seeing the world too

clearly, and this is to see, quite suddenly, the condition of your own life – with the same clarity that the first spring sunshine reveals the garden that has been obscured by winter. It makes you want to clean. It makes you – if you think of yourself as an office – want to undertake your own internal audit. You suddenly see the state of your life, not as a pose but as an accumulation.

I remember how, on my fortieth birthday, I wanted to find all the people whom I'd known when I was twenty. I wanted to photograph them all. Photography can put things to rest, I sometimes think. Recently, I found my old school photograph of the thirty or so boys who had been contemporaries; it must have been taken in the spring of 1974, a few months before we all set out to make our way in the world. We were grouped in two rows, one seated with their arms folded, the other standing behind, and we were frowning, grinning or squinting from beneath our heavy fringes towards the lens of an old plate camera. I remember the tented form of the photographer, crouching under his heavy black shroud. But the boys, and their distant faces, were like shipwrecks bleached of their history. I saw them, as it were, on a sandbank in the middle distance, a twice-thrown stone from the shore. Our final form teacher was seated in the middle of the front row, his heavy hands resting on his flannelled knees and an expression close to diffidence softening his features, as though he was daring to glance at the camera. I had not remembered his trust so coy; I remembered mostly the scent of fresh alcohol in his warm slipstream as I walked beside him and quickened my pace to his.

But I was walking towards an oubliette, which seemed to me miles wide and sunk in sour soil; I had looked down on its contours from the bedroom of my adolescence, that eternal bedroom: shrine to dreams of love and glamour, where infantilism mingled with fantasy to create a retreat from the world outside. This was at my parents' house, at the end of whose neat garden, beyond the suburban fence, subsidence was steepening the sudden escarpment into what I imagined to be *a region of myself* where it seemed inevitable that I should be forgotten.

In this sense of myself, where my feelings and my surroundings merged, this was a place of dead tracks, steel fences and a derelict school in orange brick, following the length of a smooth, grey road in bright morning sunshine, as though they were features which had been thrown from a lorry. And there they would rust and decay, in a narrow wilderness. And at the end of that grey road, I found my way to London and the office.

But today I made my way towards the new automatic doors of North Row with the strong sense that the day was somehow singled out. A season seems to me most potent in its first premature days, as it anticipates itself: a few hours of spring at the end of January, shading the dusk of the barely lengthening days the colour of damp violets; the intensity of this purple tint, occurring like a visitation, seems to charge the heady air with a low electrical current, alerting the senses but just beyond their reach. Today felt just like that; perhaps because we've had a lot of bad weather lately, and finally it was bright and mild, with fast, scudding clouds.

At North Row, I work in Brian Potter's department; I am a Deputy Group Leader (DGL) in the Silver Side team, but with no responsibilities for line management. This means, technically, that I have four assistants, but the only real distinction between us derives from my longevity of service in relation to their graduate traineeship. (The other young bunnies I mentioned when I was talking about the interview have long since left the warren.)

Anne, Kate, Perry and Dave are all about ten years younger than me, and they keep a distance from my desk which is partly a pretence of respect for seniority, but actually arises from the fact that they quite naturally prefer their own company. I find it difficult to chat with them; I was already a part of the office furniture when they arrived. With the keenness of their generation for assessing worth and status, and the concomitant disregard for anyone who doesn't embody either ambition or authority, they quickly filed me away in their heads under 'of no consequence'. But they always ask me if I'd like a coffee whenever one of them goes to get some. There was no malice in their swift judgement and subsequent disposal of my significance within the department; it was a wholly impersonal calculation of worth, based on my lack of results. Kate has a sign fastened to her work station which says, 'Second Is Nowhere'.

Our office is on the third floor. There are grey Venetian blinds over the four long windows which run at waist height along the length of one wall. The varnished wooden sill is inlaid with the slatted ducts of the air-conditioning unit. The view is of the corner of the neighbouring building, which is separated from North Row by the width of a fairly narrow street. If you stand about halfway down the office and look through the blinds at a slightly inverted angle, you can see straight through the two corner windows of the room on the fourth floor of this neighbouring building. A year or two ago, a rumour went around North Row that this corner room was used by a prostitute; then the rumour became more interesting and claimed that the room was inhabited by the odd, solitary-looking man who always seems to be in the streets around the office – not so much walking or strolling, as patrolling the area.

This particular man is short and broad, maybe in his late sixties. His head is square and his white hair is shaved down to nothing more than a patch of snowy bristles. When you pass him in the street he stops and stares at you. On the back of his head he appears to have some kind of scar, as though somebody had taken a jab at him with a potato peeler. It was perhaps because of this scar that the story evolved in the office that he has a nanotechnological chip inserted into his brain, some three eighths of an inch long, just above the pineal gland. Why these details were developed I don't know, but someone said, 'It's always near the pineal gland.'

Our office is divided across its width by a central island of chest high filing cabinets, on the top of which are two stunted yucca plants, a microfiche index and a scanner. None of these things has been touched for as long as I can remember. My team, the five of us, occupy the five desks nearest to the windows. Perry and Dave sit facing one another at one pair of desks, and Kate and Anne at another. There is a thin, barely audible bat-squeak of status in the fact that my desk stands on its own, to one side, but this could just as easily be taken for exclusion from the tribe.

Behind my right shoulder, flush to the partition wall, there is a glass-fronted cupboard which contains some old telephone directories, the two bulging, laminated ring-binders of the constantly amended Systems Procedure Manual, and an ancient bag of decaffeinated Dutch coffee which is now as hard as a rock. I bought this bag of coffee in about 1994, when I conceived of the plan to renew my relationship with the office by bringing in a few home comforts — exotic accessories, you might say.

Paul, I remember, once had a similar plan back in the Eighties. He was going to avenge himself on the fact that he worked in a particularly strait-laced department of the American Bank, by learning the Japanese tea ceremony. Spiritual hygiene was all the rage back in those days, and what with under-desk foot massage pads and phials of motivating energy oils to swab across your pulse points at regular intervals, Paul was simply keeping up to speed. But then his enthusiasm dwindled – rather because his colleagues approved – and he went back to booze. So much for cocooning; bring on the pleasure revenge.

This morning, the first thing I noticed when I came into the office was a pile of blue plastic crates stacked in the middle of the room. They were each stamped with the names Stamford and Gitting and I recognized them of old: they had the familiarity of family Christmas decorations and they meant that the Accommodation Services Department were ready to relocate us. In fact, the ASD refer to this process as 'migration'. Like a flock of sheep, we were being sent to graze for the summer on higher pastures.

The second thing I noticed, with a disproportionately savage surge of irritation, was a brown circulation envelope, placed prominently in the middle of my desk – like an accusation – and which contained, I knew, some further amendments to the Systems Procedure Manual. 'Potter,' said Kate, with a sympathetic smile when she saw me looking down at it with an expression of contempt.

I hung my jacket over the back of my chair and felt that immense fatigue which seems to weigh me down at the start of every working day. Anne was making a telephone call, laughing as she went over the details of what had happened to her the previous evening. She was comparing notes with the person on the other end of the line, and kept saying 'I didn't! I didn't!' in a tone of voice which screamed that she wanted the other person to say 'You did!'. When she finally hung up, still tittering, she looked towards Kate to share the joke, but Kate was getting ready to speak to Simon Grinch from the fourth floor, who is known as the Other Simon. Then Anne glanced at me, but looked down at her work again almost immediately, as though she had made a mistake. As with Kate's smile, when she said 'Potter' this reflexive gesture made me feel once again the chasm of indifference, or incomprehension, or differing sensibility, which separates me from my colleagues far more than the width of grey carpet which actually separates our desks. It's a shame, because I think that deep down we all want to get on.

These four assistants of mine, who attract material comfort as though by telekinesis, are tutees of last decade's Boom Economy. They have only two adjectives: 'excellent' and 'brilliant'. Anything which is neither excellent nor brilliant, in their opinions, is not worth mentioning. The confidence to pronounce sentence with such certainty has been programmed into their circuits; they have no anxiety – nor even a concept of anxiety. They know precisely where they will be in five minutes' times, five months' time and five years' time. Already, Potter is grooming the quartet for a higher calling; to be frank, nearly all of their work is of a far greater importance to the department than mine.

I just wish I could make this matter, as I sit here, cycling through air. And then it began to occur to me: maybe making this matter was why the day seemed singled out? But how do you ever know, with something as vague and as definite as a mood?

In appearance, my four assistants look as though they could be two pairs of siblings. Anne and Perry are both on the heavy side, with that lifeless brown hair which is the colour of an old fence, and slightly rounded faces. They also both have pale skin and blue eyes. They're the kind of people who you automatically assume are friendly and cheerful. When Perry uses foul language, it comes as a real shock.

Anne wears her hair in a short, sensible bob, with a side-parting and fringe held out of her eyes by a small enamelled clip. She wears a navy blue trouser suit most days, and her shirts, with their long, pointed collars, look like they are made of silk. She favours the muted shades of oyster and ivory which hover in the hinterland of off-white. Usually, she wears a necklace of fat imitation pearls, and her wristwatch is on a thin and battered strip of brown leather. It looks like it has sentimental value for her.

Perry – surname Starling – is her male equivalent. He is one of those young men whom people would describe as 'a big chap', but by their tone you would know they meant 'dependable' and 'considerate' as well. He dresses in a dark blue suit, and his wide, almost owlish features are partially hidden behind a pair of thick-lensed glasses which have heavy black frames. When he stands up he hitches up his trousers and tucks in his shirt; and again, his corporeality is taken for bonhomie, in rather the same way that some people believe that regional accents are a sure sign of honesty. But when Perry lounges behind his desk, reading some fax or other, he could almost pass for a progressive barrister.

If Anne and Perry are the sturdily studious half of the outfit, then Dave and Kate make their impression as lean, slick and self-consciously physical. To see them together, you would suppose that they were one of those couples whose long-standing relationship is based, above all, on their physical similarity to one another. Both are fair, with lightly tanned, unblemished skin; both are tall, with trim, slender figures. Kate, in fact, is Dave with small breasts. Here are born leaders: nature's prefects, with loud, confident voices and the self-assurance to express their feelings on any subject without fear of the consequences.

They are both the type of person who seem to enjoy the best of all worlds, and this is what makes them seem so modern: three times a week they both go off to their exercise classes, following one another out of the office with their branded sports bags. And ninety minutes later they both return showered and radiant, their strong white teeth bared in happy grins. But then they both smoke American low tar cigarettes with the confidence of people who know that they will never fall foul of addiction: they are healthy smokers, luxuriating in their well-being.

Kate and Dave flirt with one another, constantly, in that particularly public manner of flirtation which takes the form of their ceaselessly and delightedly insulting, chaffing and smacking one another. It is as though they cannot wait to go to bed together but are locked in a foreplay of sparring which heightens their desire for one another, even as it expresses their ecstatic frustration at the constraints which they have placed on their relationship. Neither one of them, it seems, is going to give the other the satisfaction of hearing them ask for more. Such is their bondage, which they must find mutually erotic; the office, after all, is a pressure cooker of lust, cooking up collusion through confinement.

Dave is perfectly clear as to what his ideal lover would look like. The subject came up one afternoon — it was a Friday — in one of those meandering conversations which can occur in the office towards the end of the day. I don't remember what the rest of them had to say on the subject but I was struck by Dave's precision: 'Sun-bed blonde in a black BMW,' he announced, 'with a Dalmatian.' And I knew exactly what he had in mind; it was such an effortless object of desire, as easy as putting a square peg in a square hole.

Kate, in many ways, is the terrestial reflection of Dave's ideal; of course, she can never be as curvacious, complicit and cooingly aroused as the dream blonde of his imagination, but it is her close proximity to the fantasy which has given her teasing such erotic staying power. I feel sure that she has become the embodiment of lust for Dave.

Perry looks on with an expression which alternates between wolfish, sharkish and sheepish; he listens to Dave as though he was watching him beat someone up. Kate fades in and out of their conversation like an electric current on a weak rural circuit, her sensuality flickering in the twilight of their frustration. And Anne, less self-assured, becomes increasingly busy with her paperwork – the more she pretends to be amused. She thought that the bit about the Dalmatian was a real hoot.

It had just occurred to me that it would be Simon Grinch who would finally reel in Kate on his sticky line of compliments, and then Dave swung through the door and dropped another brown circulation envelope on to my desk. They were collecting for someone's party.

'Frankie downstairs,' — Dave got the name out before I could ask, pronouncing 'downstairs' as though it was Frankie's surname: 'Frankie Downstairs.' 'And Irene,' he added.

The envelope hit my desk with a thump, which indicated rather too much small change for either Frankie or Irene to feel certain of their popularity. I held the envelope open on my desk and peered inside. These envelopes are always slightly damp and coarse to the touch; their grids of address boxes recount their journey around the office, in signatures and acronyms. They seem to use the oldest envelopes for these collections; half filled with money, they smell like cold metal in a dusty drawer.

At a glance, there was maybe sixty quid in one and two pound coins, with a few lordly tenners from those in upper management whose generosity would otherwise be missed. I remember that I dropped in my two quid at a little after twenty to ten. I got up from my desk to take the envelope over to Kate, but she was still in a deep conversation with Simon which seemed to involve a lot of soft phrases and lowered eyes. She didn't so much as glance at me, but just as I was sitting down again she peeped out from behind Simon, smiled and said 'Thanks'.

I had put off the moment when I would have to go

through the loathesome System Amendments, partly because I have never been quite sure what exactly I'm meant to do with them, and partly because there are always six other jobs which need doing as well. I guessed that Frankie Downstairs and Irene would be getting the usual send off: a party which began in the office and then travelled over the road to the Marlborough, a pub whose fittings are an epic of fake Victoriana, clamped together by the brute grey casing of six wide-screen TVs.

The Marlborough stands on a corner in the narrow no man's land between the bustle of Oxford Street and the stillness of Mayfair's secretive mansion blocks. The pub was always supposed to be a pick-up joint for the last of Green Street's prostitutes but I find that hard to believe. These days it's mostly tourists and men in suits like myself. But Barry Who Left used to say, in his rasping, villainous voice 'They're girls on casework, that's what they are', meaning that the women met their clients with the accessories of fetish carried with them in a little case.

I cannot repeat too often: sex obsesses the office. And when I worked in the City, it was more than an obsession. Sex seemed to be in the air that they breathed and the coffee they drank. On warm summer days, from Blackfriars to Moorgate lust and exhaust seemed to cook together in the hot streets.

I feel ashamed when I think about Barry Who Left,

because I believe that he wanted to be my friend and I found his friendship a burden. When a colleague wants to start a friendship, you've suddenly got a new responsibility. Barry and I met during a low period in his life. His father was dying and Barry himself was trying to do a course at night school. He valued my opinion on life's changes.

Today, Barry seems like a character from another era; as archaic and remote, as quaint, even, as an interviewee in a television documentary from the early Seventies. But even in the middle of the 1980s, he looked old-fashioned in a particularly distinctive way. At that time, for a young man of twenty-seven to be wearing colour-coordinated matching shirt and tie combinations – the collars of the shirts being double-stitched and rounded – with grey slacks and side-zipped boots, was neither normal nor fashionable. It simply looked odd; and yet Barry was oblivious to its oddness.

On other days, he would wear lace-up brogues in two-tone leather of cream and navy blue; his sharp-looking suits were made out of obscure synthetics which might have been some mutant polyester which had originated as a chemical bi-product in the manufacture of bubble wrap. He had the hairstyle of a cabaret singer from an out-of-the-way, middle European city: the controlled explosion of his fringe gave way to two carefully combed back wings of hair, which just clipped the lobes of his ears before coming to rest, at the back, just over the collar of his jacket.

Despite this, Barry had a natural stylishness which touched on glamour. He existed outside the Zeitgeist, embodying the deepest sincerity. Incapable of affectation, even in his performances for me, as the old lag who knew the ropes, he was driven by a fundamental generosity which I had nothing to deserve.

So why did I let him down? Why did I find his very friendliness a strain and approach our lunches together – a pub sandwich or a burger wolfed down beneath the despotically bright lights of a basement seating area – with a sinking heart?

In addition to the gyratory of hatred, there is the orbital of embarrassment. These two systems are connected by the slip roads of ingested feelings. But once on the loop of embarrassment, you cannot recall a single occasion on which you have not been either embarrassed or embarrassing. With Barry, I think that I was embarrassed because he was performing for me. His role was the straight-talker: a toned-down version of Martin from Waste, in fact. And I always seem to let myself become an audience. This must be an intimacy regulator, which I have only switched off in my dealings with one or two people, and then a long time ago.

Between Barry and myself, the relationship between the audience and the performer had become confused;

and my embarrassment – often it feels more like shame, or a shared sorrow for the both of us – could be compared to that of a person who was called up on stage, as a volunteer, to a stunt that went wrong.

I only met Barry's girlfriend once and I have forgotten her name. This meeting must have taken place about twelve years ago, but it seems in recollection to be an episode from another life. Barry was devoted to his girlfriend (her name might have been Clare) and he had spoken about her so much to me that when we were finally introduced there was something unreal about being brought into her actual presence.

The meeting took place in spring. I can picture the blue evening light; the pavement looking scrubbed clean against the tubs of pale yellow daffodils which were standing outside the pub in South Audley Street.

Clare was sitting on a tapestry-covered bar stool beside one of those black, heavily varnished pub tables; she wasn't particularly tall, and she looked more boyish, in frame and figure, than petite or pert; her dark brown hair was cut short above the collar of her white shirt. She was even wearing the brown suede skirt which Barry had once described to me. With her knees pressed tightly together, and her hands resting in her lap, I got the impression that she was from a wealthier and better educated background than Barry; that his apparent roughness and her inherited gentility were the opposing qualities which had attracted them to one another.

And perhaps this was why, when we shook hands, I felt that there was something slightly defensive about her manner; it was almost as though she was afraid that I would think she was from the same social drawer as her boyfriend. This, at any rate, is what happens when certain people meet one another for the first time, in a situation which might compromise their vanity; there is an exchange, albeit in code, and albeit unwillingly, to assert that we are conscious of our rank. Like the attitudes of the City's Old Guard, this trait has lingered on, but in disguise.

I think that Barry must have built me up to his girlfriend as an 'interesting character'. She seemed to be on her best behaviour. Once the declarations of status had concluded between us — but on such a high frequency of social intercourse that only our attuned senses were alert to their transmission — Clare was now eager to please Barry by appearing eager to like me. In a sudden shift of roles, I had become the performer to her audience; and I was painfully aware, within minutes of sitting down in the quiet, twilit pub, of just how clumsily and to what little entertaining effect I assumed the command that this shift entailed. Clare's politeness was all too apparent, when, egged on by Barry, I tried to give a funny description of the man with a nanotechnological microchip in his brain.

Barry, meanwhile, had become a different person from the moment the three of us had met. He was standing directly behind his girlfriend's chair as she and I shook hands; and as she had remained seated, looking up at me with a wide-mouthed smile, Barry had seemed to dance from side to side behind her, monitoring her comfort with an attentiveness and anxiety which took the form of his making little patting gestures around her arms and shoulders, as though he didn't quite dare to disturb her with his touch – or, rather, that he was keeping an eye on some precious aura which existed around the outline of her body. You can have your aura massaged, you know.

At the time I didn't particularly envy them their relationship; looking after Clare seemed like a full-time job to me. But to Barry she was a remarkable person – life-giving, in his eyes – and she rewarded him with little snippets of intimacy. I got the impression that when she sulked it would be impossible to imagine her sunny and generous – just as her happier moods would confound the idea that she could ever become bad tempered or depressed. It was this absence of a middle ground which made me fear for Barry's peace of mind.

When I look at my four assistants, whom I would like to feel some warmth towards, I see them as representatives of a generation rather than as individuals. They seem to exist as a dumping ground for clichés;

they live in a culture of superlatives, which is based entirely on sampling the most exaggerated elements from everything. But looted from their context, these elements have become meaningless, save as signifiers of some idea of the extreme. As starved of imagination as it is gorged on self-confidence, this gener—

'We'd better use 404.'

Brian Potter's voice boomed through the office; I looked up from my desk, where the inserts for the Systems Amendments were fanned out like the slices of melon in a steak house starter, and caught a glimpse of Potter's heavy frame, pulling away from the door. He is a big man: tall, broad and powerfully built; his shirts seem to stretch across the shifting packs of muscle of his chest and back. He embodies dynamism; he clicks his fingers as he walks down the corridor, swaggering slightly. Prior to Potter's promotion, our immediate boss was a ferret-like man who kept himself to himself, and slunk around the building as though he was trespassing. His name was Mr Figg, or 'Syrup'.

'Well. We all know what this'll be about,' said Perry, picking up a spiral-bound notepad and pulling on his jacket.

'Item One: Relocation,' said Simon Grinch, who had not been sure whether or not Potter had seen him hanging around Kate's desk. 'We've already been told about it. You'll have to start packing up your stuff this afternoon . . .'

Kate groaned and rubbed her face with the palms of her hands. 'I'm just too busy, right now, to be playing around with all of this.'

Simon, sensing the mood had changed, withdrew. 'See you later,' he said, and tapped the corner of her desk with his knuckle as he turned to leave.

'Yeah. See you later . . .' The iron core of professionalism had returned to Kate's tone. My assistants, as I have said, express the entire range of their emotions in two states of mind: ecstatic or sulking. Now, they were all sulking. 'Can I put my calls through to Louise?' asked Anne. And as she spoke, I felt the patch of freezing numbness, about the side of a postage stamp, just above my left eye. It seems to happen a lot these days: one of the several symptoms which have been conspiring to disturb me; symptoms which I never seemed to having during those blue spring evenings, over a decade ago, when characters like Barry were still around.

Leaving the office with the rest of them, to make our way to the conference room, 404, I felt ashamed and unattractive for disliking the attitudes of a younger generation, for even thinking in those terms. And when I think of Barry and his girlfriend – of those hurried lunches in basement seating areas – it seems so long ago. Everything seems to piss me off these days, and then my left eye goes numb.

Room 404 is sometimes used for private lunches

by the upper management; as a consequence of this, it has a savoury odour. There are long sideboards down the length of one wall, which contain ingeniously concealed hotplates. Perry once found a bottle of Bailey's Irish Cream in one of the cupboards. Today, twelve stackable chairs – moulded orange plastic with black metal legs – were arranged loosely around the long table. Anne half opened one of the vertical blinds, saying 'That's better' when the room became brighter.

Derek and Liam, from Accommodation Services, were already sitting at one end of the table, their jackets off and their sleeves rolled up. Liam's pointed chin is covered by a neatly clipped beard which emphasizes the thinness of his lips; he also wears those big, square-framed glasses which seem to be popular with technically-minded people. Derek, a burly Cockney, has the air of a pop group's road manager; the moment he sits down, he takes his pager off his belt, looks at it, and then puts it down on the table in front of him. His technique in meetings is impressive; Armaggedon could just have been announced, and he would say, 'Be that as it may, I'm going to have thirty people without desks, and they're all going to be ringing me up. Or Dave, of course . . .' Dave being Derek's deputy. As we sat down, Liam gave us an ironic smile but Derek's expression didn't flicker.

I took a seat at the far corner of the table, stretching out my legs and putting my hands in my pockets. The room felt warm and the grey carpet seemed to rob it of air. There was a strong smell of vending machine coffee wafting in from the corridor. Two lovers, by Chagall (wearing floral crowns as they floated over Paris) looked down on us with dreamy eyes from behind their covering of plexiglass. The walls of Room 404 are hung with a beige-coloured fabric — imitation slub silk, at a guess. The place has the air of a disused thoroughfare, always feeling empty even when there are people in there.

Potter marched in and took his place at the head of the table; he glanced around to check that we had all turned up. Here was a man with no time to waste on the preliminary niceties; a man forged in the furnace of the enterprise economy and then plunged to harden in the freezing waters of the recession. He began to speak, and my mind began to wander; first through the thickets of my immediate concerns, and then . . .

'Right. This is going to be a nuisance for all of us, and it would help enormously if you could just —'

Is it the office which has held me down, and which reduces me to exploring those fantasies which serve as a substitute for living? At forty, they say, the soul is stopped and questioned; hope and fear must fight it out, or reason the way ahead. My fear, and it must be common, is that I have an alien on board; my hope —

FOUR

Brian Potter's voice — mannered yet declamatory, a rhythm of decisiveness — reached my end of the table as if with the three second delay which you used to experience on satellite telephone calls. Then, as I began to drift, warm and relaxed, between sluggish consciousness and a restful doze, the stresses in Potter's phrasing assumed a regularity which kept time with my breathing, and took on the resonance of a chanted 'om'. This seemed to aid the evacuation of troublesome thoughts from my mind and clear the ground for messages of enlightenment.

I was neither asleep nor awake; and I was entering a state which was as far removed from sorrow as it was from common cheerfulness. But although I was experiencing the sensation of sinking into myself, I feel sure that had I been called to attention on a point of procedure I would have been able to give a lucid answer. It was as though a stage in my mind had been set and lit, for the unhindered enactment of a particular drama.

I was always so clear, in my youth, about where and how I wanted to live. It began with straight lines. I was raised, aesthetically, on the Ladderex shelving and steel-lined corridors which signified a global headquarters in the secret agent television series of the middle to late Sixties. You could say that I cut my teeth on the glamour of an office where the business of international espionage – on the administrative side, at any rate – was conducted amidst the same quiet efficiency that you might expect in the executive departments of any major corporation.

Other than the works of Titus Petronius Arbiter, the only book which made a real impression on me, and which I carried around with me, throughout my nineteenth summer, was William H. Whyte's *The Organization Man*. To me, this book spelled out the business of living, as allegory or analysis, and I used to reread Whyte's closing sentences with the same fervour that another boy might have felt as he finished *On The Road*. Whyte's concluding pronouncement on the fate of the office worker was a tract I learned by heart: 'It is wretched, dispiriting advice to hold before him the dream that ideally there is no conflict between him and society. There always is; there always must be. Ideology cannot wish it away; the peace of mind offered by organization remains a surrender, and no less so for being offered in benevolence. That is the problem.' There followed, in my edition, an Appendix: 'How To Cheat On Personality Tests'.

With regard to the brushed metal and mirror-glassed world of secret agents, I was in love with these sophisticated, multilingual men who dressed in single-breasted mohair suits and always finished one another's sentences with an air of ironic yet sturdy camaraderie. I loved the elegant way that they sipped their black coffee in the depths of leather sofas, while their crotchety but paternal Controller – bushy-eyebrowed in tweed – would brief them on the doings of the latest villainous Turk. Back in those days, the enemy was so apparent.

As a child of the surburbs, enamoured less by the suave violence of these secret agents than by their neatness – their side partings, their attaché cases, their short wave biros – I used to draw pictures of sleek office fittings, cut them out and stick them on to my bedroom wall. These were the emblems of a covert superiority: a power described by straight lines which was the modern expression of dandyism.

I would gaze towards the high-rise skyline of Croydon – compared, from the air, to mid-town Johannesburg – and dream about the space race office blocks of Luna House, Apollo House and Zodiac House. Today, demonized and dreary, these three-decade-old towers have an air of abandonment, even though they're still in use. When I was a child, they promised The Life.

But this appreciation was a balancing act, even then; because I also loved the pastel pastoral of our modest suburban garden and the wilderness beyond the fence . . . To this day, sunlight on suburban lawns makes me think of the loneliness of a suburb betrayed: that the innocence of those loyal gardens was exchanged to chase the glamour of a concrete vista, and that in wanting both, both were lost.

I'm too ready, I often think, to assess my life in terms of loss; and that is what I want to redress: romantics are always looking back, trying to recapture the split second of infinite potential, before their dream was circumscribed.

Back in 1976, Paul had a girlfriend who called herself Christine Kleenex; a chunky seventeen-year-old, she had cut off most of her hair with a pair of kitchen scissors and dyed what remained the murky blue of school ink. She lived with her younger sister and elder brother on one of the big estates which you can still see from the District Line as the train rattles east beyond Mile End. Her parents never seemed to be at home.

Christine's style and maturity put me in awe of her. I see myself then: a lanky eighteen-year-old with thin wrists and a drooping, unkissed mouth. None of my clothes fitted me properly because I was so skinny, and I had no style at all − just a map of style, which I knew by heart, and added to daily. Christine Kleenex would travel on the bus dressed in a black leotard, fishnet tights and a bubble-gum pink translucent plastic mac. She had changed her surname to Kleenex and scrawled 'BIG SISTER IS WATCHING YOU' across the window of a sex shop in King's Cross. She took no notice whatsoever when Paul or myself tried to play the rebel.

I was thrown by this, having hoped that the three

of us would represent some sort of solidarity; instead, Christine's comments cut the legs from under any cosy stance of assumed superiority. I must have resented the way in which she did this, but because I admired her so much I never argued.

She stayed with Paul for nearly two years. But while Paul and myself were bewitched by the grey twilight of punk, always hoping for some new piece of music which could sum up our experience of wandering around London, looking through other people's windows, Kleenex abandoned the whole thing, including her re-invented surname. She started training to become a psychiatric nurse.

Paul started drinking heavily. I mistook his despair for worldly alienation, and then I watched him disappear beneath the surface of the crowd in that pub in Holborn. How do couples break up? It always seems to be the same, when you get down to it. A wet night; a street of terraced houses. Somebody you don't know's party. Telephones.

These memories felt as though they had always been with me, and yet I couldn't recall having thought about Christine for years. My thoughts took me back to the earliest days of the office, and to the train journey from West Croydon to London Bridge; I recalled the way the landscape changed, from the endless house backs and overgrown Edwardiana of the outer suburbs, on through Forest Hill and Anerley, to the sudden opening out of London proper, beyond New Cross: the sprawling estates which flank the south side of the river, beneath a sky which looked too big, past Millwall FC and the old City Mission, on to London Bridge station.

This was before the station was rebuilt; today, the concourse smells of hot plastic and laminated paper; then, it still had the smell of soot and cinders, and the airless, musty scent of the old British Rail upholstery. And as the passengers disembarked, they seemed to be translated from one state to another; for me, that moment of translation was the pulse of The Life.

In my early twenties, already tethered to the office, I longed to be a dandyfied urban anthropologist – hence Petronius and *The Organization Man*. Part secret agent, part social scientist, I would become, by the sheer acuity of my perceptions, both aristocratic and armoured. And my dandyism would be the subtle articulation of this position. This was very different to simply fancying myself as an aesthete: an aesthete, generally, is a person who contemplates single objects in otherwise empty rooms. I wanted to study the whole city. Similarly, I don't think that I had any notion of urban anthropologists as an academic breed, lurking in university departments, growing embittered about the reception of their footnotes.

My idea of urban anthropology was much better: besuited romanticism. A placer of the details of modern city life beneath the microscope of informed scrutiny. You could call it a form of heightened naturalism, or progressive lucidity – the sort of vision which enables you to survey society as an independent observer and chart its every twitch.

This would be the reverse, in many ways, of being the psychic lightning conductor: more of a scanner to catch every bleap and squeak of the Zeitgeist. In another sense, I would have been like a geologist, but charting the contours and strata of status, not land. If everything was turning into the idea and image of itself, then I would respond, in turn, by describing every progenitor and medium of that imagery *as a type* – classifiable, disarmed. (With regard to the arts, it would be elementary that the only culture that's ever successful, as cultural commodity, is the culture which flatters the temper of the Zeitgeist at any given time – wacky, dreamy, dopey, gritty, whatever.)

As befitted my status and autonomy, I would of course be luxuriously housed in some fold of metropolitan blueness: down by the river, somewhere between Tower Bridge and Greenwich Pier. The block would be a fifteen-storey Brutalist tower, its balconied windows the same matt green as the Thames at high tide; the slabs of prestressed concrete would make a feature of their raw ridges, coated with chippings of glistening flint. And from my big apartment on the top floor I would be the analyst and synthesist of all that I surveyed; comprehending the immensity of the human condition by knowing why people shopped alone, or wore loud ties or citric perfume, or started taking exercise, or preferred a natural finish on their furnishings. And then I would have won.

This little dream, of ascending from the drudgery of clerical life to a heightened, independent state of operation, most probably saw me through the best part of a decade. I was always preparing for the role, rehearsing my masterpiece as I swayed and lurched with the other standing passengers on the underground between Bond Street and the Bank, or wandered around the shops in my lunch hour. I envisaged myself as a vital witness to events – not just another office worker dressed in the battle fatigues of his cheap suit, daily put through the assault course of commuting, taunted by adverts which played upon his dreams and frustration. I would become a sculptor who worked in demographics, trend, and image.

I would always appear smart, sleek and alert – advancing masked, disguised by Savile Row, *'because one should dress and behave like a bourgeois in order to be violent and original in one's work'*. I would develop a method of commentary, as witty as it was perspicacious, through which I would refine my analysis of an urban subject from a paragraph, to a sentence, to a single word; and with that single word I would define the countenance of an era.

Like distant drumming, I could hear my assistant, Perry, becoming more and more heated as he explained to Potter and his nodding colleagues why the disruption caused by this office 'migration' could not have come at a worse time. I frowned and nodded also; Potter happened to glance at me, and our frowns met along the length of the table. He had approved of my frown, which was why he too had frowned, our eyes meeting. It was an exchange of looks which could have accompanied us holding hands for the first time.

On the other side of the street, someone opened a window; the morning sunshine was suddenly reflected off the new angle of the window pane, and an oblong of golden light took its place on the wall of Room 404, just beneath a corner of the ceiling. The light trembled, as though it was coming off the surface of a swimming pool. As I watched it, I suddenly realized how thin and worn my fantasy of becoming an urban anthropologist had become.

And this came as quite a jolt. It was like entering a familiar room with fresh eyes, and seeing how shabby and faded the paintwork and furnishings have become. In the past, whenever I had perused the landscape of my ambition with an eye to enshrining the eloquence of minutiae, I would come home in my fantasy to a view of London – 'and now you and I come to grips!' But now I found that the purpose of this role – authority, control, power – had become obscure. Little by little, the sheen of glamour had dulled, and the slick, taut dynamics of my persona had begun to slacken. Where once I had imagined an *über*-analyst, synthesizing the chaos of impressions, I now wanted more. Or less. But what?

The beginnings of the answer seemed to lie in that trembling patch of sunshine on the wall of Room 404. I saw in its lateral associations of promise a new set of questions. Increasingly, I worry about terminal illness, waiting to declare itself. And then I spend a lot of time considering the nature of success and failure: how are they constituted, and what must it be like to be at ease with your achievements?

So now my habitual self was being questioned by a new set of concerns; it was as though the decisions which I had taken during adolescence, to become a certain sort of person, were approaching their date for renewal; as though an audit had occurred and a bill had fallen due. To put it another way, you can only rehearse your masterpiece for so long.

By now, Kate had come up with an idea for access to storage; Dave wanted to know why the doors to our office were actually going to be sealed. Room 404, under the influence of that patch of reflected sunshine, appeared suddenly filled with summer. My colleagues had settled in for a long haul through the state of the office. My detachment deepened; I felt as though I was lucid dreaming –

Despite the warmth of the long weekend, a sabbath

stillness hung over the empty platforms, mingling with the heat haze at their furthest end, beyond the dust-coloured shadow of the station's high roof. Squinting against the glare of the morning sun, I looked down the tracks as they stretched away, the faint curve of the rails reflecting a white light as bright as burning magnesium. Back towards the echoing concourse, the digits on the station clocks were flicking over with their steady metallic click . . .

Dreaming of Victoria Station, I dreamed that I would be meeting the girl I had seen outside the coffee bar this morning – grey eyes, unimpeachable honesty, the bringer of cool water! Even though I've had girlfriends in the past, as I said, relationships and sex are things which only seem to happen in my head now. You just don't meet new people. But I like to think that I have an instinctive respect for women: that no matter how much a woman might appeal to me on a purely sensual level, I will always distinguish the appreciation of her mind and character as two exams to be passed with flying colours. The trouble is, I don't know how to flirt, and when I used to try I came across as some kind of freak. Paul told me that this was why women avoided me like the plague. 'You don't hold their interest and you don't make them laugh,' he said, 'so they smile at your politeness, find it suspicious and then turn back to their friends.'

I also have the unhappy knack of making women

feel ugly. When they are with me, women find that their clothes suddenly seem ridiculous and ill-fitting; they start tugging at the seams of their skirts, trying to cover themselves up and distract all attention from their appearance.

This is why I settled, in the end, for the role of the couple's dependable friend; I had felt that I was 'By Appointment', so to speak, to scores of couples – to Paul and Christine, Barry and Clare, countless others, over the years. If people – other than Paul – ever came to like me, it was usually because I either flattered them by asking them lots of questions about their life and achievements, or because I took an interest in their relationships. It has reinforced couples' sense of partnership, also, to look upon me as their surrogate son: the men all full of advice, the women all gossipy and maternal. I have been castrated, in fact, by my role in other people's relationships.

Over the years I have felt my most passionate experience of love for strangers whom I have only seen in coffee shops, or on trains, or shopping during their lunch hours. In fact, I have felt this passion more for the places which remind me of those strangers, than for the people themselves. It is as though those places – the concourse coffee shop, an aisle in a department store, a particular exit from the underground – are the most intense refinement of those dreams of love: the concentrate, the essence. Which is why I'm all for

99

perfumes which smell of particular places. They could do different versions for the different times of day, as well: 'Evening In Bond Street', 'Debenhams at Noon', 'Last Train'.

When Paul went out of circulation, I used to go to a little café in Victoria Street, just beside the entrance to Artillery Mansions. In those days, Artillery Mansions was a sombre edifice of red brick, indented with the mean slits of a hundred dirty windows which looked as though they only admitted a brown stain of light. An arch like a yawning mouth led into a dark courtyard. It was the kind of place where disgraced civil servants committed suicide.

The little café was called the New Era; it always seemed to be winter when I went there. I don't think the place had changed since 1959: scalding cups of watery tea and coffee were dispensed from a massive stainless steel urn on the counter; each table had a tasselled, taffeta lampshade which gave off a feeble crimson light and an odour of burnt dust; tiles of black and white lino covered the floor. The walls were mostly bare, except for the metal outline of a guitar, and a picture of the Bay of Naples — Vesuvius through the mist, the elegant curve of the promenade.

There used to be a time when the city was my erotic theatre: when a good-looking, unobtainable woman would be synonymous with the city itself. Walking the smarter streets at sunset — St James's, Mayfair —

I found nothing banal, in those days, about the notion of some New Helen who would embody the romance of the London evening: the reflection of candlelight in gilded mirrors, and the scarlet gleam of brake lights in the gathering dusk.

And as I walked, glimpsing the settings for other people's love affairs, I dreamed up a cast of beauties who were all the same woman: serious, sensual, reserved, yet capable of flexing the toned muscles of their sexuality, just enough to reveal a taste for licentiousness. In short, I was no more refined than my assistant, Dave, with his sun-bed blonde in a black BMW.

But the office runs on fantasy, as surely as it runs on lust and coffee and cheese salad sandwiches; there must be scores of detailed fantasies accompanying the labelling of envelopes and the typing out of correspondence and the repagination of updated documents. Dreams of how to live with renewed status, dreams of requited love or downright lust, dreams of telling the sharp-tongued boss just where he can stuff his job. And all the while, your work before you, fuelling the fantasy. And that's how They control Us.

As Potter droned on, I dreamed I was back in the New Era café. Seated at the end of the conference table, with my eyes half shut (shielded by the flat of my hand, as though I was leaning forward to concentrate) I could see the taffeta-shaded lamps, and the long street-facing window with the dimming light of a winter's afternoon pressing against it. Sunday again. I was the only customer.

It would have been typical, in such a daydream at the office, for me to conjure up some promise of romance, the young woman from outside the coffee bar on Victoria Station, for instance. But when I tried — thinking of grey eyes and the look of unimpeachable honesty — all I saw were real women: the women of Victoria Station. I saw rolled magazines stuffed down the sides of bulging canvas bags; I pictured their hurried walk across the crowded concourse, heads lowered. I recalled the tired, irritable, resigned faces; scuffed heels, Silk Cut, the instinct not to make eye contact with anyone. No sirens there, to lure the lonely clerk to his doom on mirrored rocks.

Not to be able to fantasize alarmed me.

Back in the New Era café, I had already paid my bill. It was late afternoon. Outside it was freezing hard. I turned into the backstreets of Westminster, where the pale façades of institutional buildings appeared like shuttered fortresses. Government offices, chartered association headquarters; anonymous blocks with blank, black windows and a feeble light left burning in the vestibule.

The pavements had been cleared of snow, but dirtied drifts and crusts of ice clung to the edges of steps and curbstones. There was nobody else to be seen or heard.

The cold amplified the sound of my footsteps in the empty street. Once, in summer, I would have imagined a hundred affairs between these buildings. Youth and smiles; evenings and weekends planned; seascape and sunset calling travellers and lovers, all the way from Sorrento and *bella Napoli*! The June evening sky, over St James's Park, behind me, violet and serene. But now, nothing.

Empty streets and empty buildings; darkness and cold. It seemed to me that all the sirens, and their lovers, had suddenly grown out of the business of romance. The dinner tables were deserted, the candles finally snuffed. No more teased-up hair, high heels, glittering dresses and false eyelashes; no more taxis hailed from the curb by couples encased in a cloud of Chanel. It was all over. The time demanded a new desire; a new fantasy to keep you going, throughout the long afternoon to five.

The daydream thinned in a rising clamour of voices, the pushing back of chairs and the sound of Brian Potter saying something about amendments. Perry was laughing in a forced, hearty way, as though Potter was the greatest deliverer of dry wisecracks who had ever lived. I could no longer see the patch of trembling sunlight, just beneath the corner of the ceiling; the sun had inched its way around the building, or been covered by a cloud. We all trooped out of the conference room.

I glanced back into the empty room and thought I saw the ghost of an urban anthropologist. In the corridor, people were leaving for lunch.

FIVE

'The weather today just can't make up its mind.'

The woman speaking – I think her name is Maureen – was just ahead of me, making her way to the central staircase with another woman, whose name I don't know. Maureen is a few years past fifty, I would have thought. Her hair is dyed gold, and when it isn't piled on top of her head, held in place by what look like two ebony combs and a pair of chopsticks, it must reach down to her shoulders.

Maureen is a heavy smoker. She has a deep, rasping voice and her cough is more like a bark. Every year she gets another bad attack of bronchitis. 'You could set your watch by it,' as Anne once said. But you know when Maureen's around because you can always smell the sweet, cloying perfume that she wears; it lingers for a good twenty minutes after she's gone, as well.

Like her companion, Maureen was wearing a black, knee-length skirt, a lambswool sweater in a pale pastel shade, and a cardigan thrown over her shoulders. Today, Maureen's cardigan was a vivid royal blue and her friend's a bright scarlet. Making their way to lunch, the two women both walked with their arms folded across their chests, and their purse in one hand.

As I have said, when I first arrived at North Row there used to be a lot of women like Maureen working in the Registry. Condescended to by the male, upper stratum of management, and regarded with thinly veiled impatience by those female managers who were getting caught up in the cyclone of New Professionalism, these women of early retirement age were the last connection to an earlier era of the office. In particular, they were unmoved by the reinvention of North Row. It wasn't that they opposed the sweeping changes or rose up as one in defiance of the grey carpets. But, in fact, their dismissal of the innovations could not have been more wounding to those in charge: they simply humoured them. They considered the latest fetish for information technology to be best treated in the same way they would a small nephew who was brandishing a new toy: they smiled and nodded and then turned back to their own concerns.

This drove the management white with fury. And so most of Maureen's peers – in a blizzard of brown circulation envelopes, Black Forest gateaux and brightly coloured cards – were replaced by computers. Maureen herself remained, to be championed by management as a human mascot of the heart and spine of North Row: 'Now wherever would we be without old Maureen, eh?'

Each floor of North Row is divided down its middle by a long corridor, at either end of which are a pair of double swing-doors. All of these corridors are identical, with the central staircase running down their western end; through the swing-doors, there is a kind of T-junction to further sets of offices and a service lift. Because of the staircases and swing-doors, the only natural light which reaches these corridors comes from the opened doors of their adjoining offices. These office doors are heavy, teak-effect affairs, with brushed metal finger-plates and stylish handles; the handles, in fact, remind me of swollen commas. They were a significant detail of North Row's corporate face lift; somebody told me that they echo the typography of the redesigned letterhead on the general correspondence notepaper.

The only other feature on these doors – and the doors are heavy, yielding only to an assertive pull against the pressure of their hydraulic hinges – are their narrow windows, inlaid with a grid of thin wires, placed to one side of the finger-plates. But these strips of armoured glass are especially designed to filter out daylight, and this is why the corridors are filled with the flat, toneless luminescence which comes from the bevelled planks of heat-resistant perspex that are set into the ceiling. Pristine, all of these features and fittings are like sculpture.

It is only when the doors along the corridor are opened that you suddenly get an impression, often false, of what the weather is doing. When the light in the corridor changes in this manner, I find that the effect can radically alter my mood. I have been dropped into a disproportionate fury by a sudden suggestion from the light that the sunshine of a false spring has been usurped by the monotonous cloud of an enduring winter. Similarly, I have found myself thinking of autumn in May by a received impression of soaring blue and golden skies.

But today Maureen was right: the weather just couldn't make up its mind.

I dropped back into the office to let people know I was going to lunch. Because of Potter's meeting, the morning seemed to have passed unusually quickly. Lunch can be taken at any time between the core office hours of twelve and two. You are allowed the usual hour, but most people take seventy minutes, making their own calculations about why they aren't robbing the company of nearly one hour's worth of their paid employment per working week.

I was probably thinking about something along these lines as I leaned forward to collect my jacket. And this was when the first real disturbance of the day seemed to happen. There's not much to describe about it. I was looking at Kate, who was touching up her eyeshadow in a little mirror that was balanced on her keyboard; then, I felt a shift in my perception, like a jolt to my nervous system, which was accompanied by the sensation that I had lost my short-term memory. It was as though the day no longer existed as an accumulation of its lived hours and my experience of its informants. At the same time, I suddenly felt distanced from my surroundings, as though I was seeing everything through a thick sheet of glass. Combined, these effects became a mixture of feelings – panic and emptiness. But I smiled at Kate, picked up my jacket and went back out into the corridor. I just felt odd, and wanted to distract myself from the oddness.

On my way downstairs I saw Simon Grinch coming up to our office. He grinned at me as we passed one another, and I tried to remember which artist was described as having phallic teeth. Simon was taking the stairs two at a time, pulling himself up by the bannister with his right hand, and making the whole ascent bent double, at an urgent, lolloping run. He has blond, slicked-back hair, a thin, gaunt face and a pointed chin. His eyes are pale blue, with a piercing expression. He is considered quite a pin-up.

Outside, the earlier sunshine had disappeared beneath vast continents of grey cloud; the gaps between them, through which you could still see patches of blue sky, had the appearance of land-locked seas. A chilly wind had got up, sweeping around the corners of the buildings in swift, persistent gusts, blowing people's coats around them and pressing them forward as they walked, as though with a push in the back. I crossed the street with my hands in my pockets and my shoulders hunched.

The office at North Row is close enough to Oxford Street to feel the clamour of the West End's busy thoroughfare. As soon as you leave the building you are caught by the quickening current of the atmosphere:

the queues of traffic and buses, stretching from Marble Arch to Centre Point. On hot summer days it looks like a cattle drive. Today, with panic and emptiness still marking time with my footsteps, I welcomed the familiarity of the roaring lunch hour.

The people on the streets looked like representatives from many different eras: from the present, young men from neighbouring offices, many of them little more than teenagers, sauntered down the pavement in two and threes. Swaggering in their suits and ties, healthy and happy, they seemed to be looking over the heads of the crowds towards some goal on the near horizon that was their private kingdom. Young women, alone or in scurrying pairs, contributed their urgency to the vitality of this procession, which is at once intent and meandering, simultaneously vague yet precise.

From the near future, there was a boy in a dirty silver anorak; his sports shoes had anarchy symbols drawn on their rubberized toecaps. Behind him there was a young man wearing a waistcoat of moss-green suede, which was worn down to black leather along its creases; under this, a purple scoop-necked T-shirt. His jeans were frayed and faded. He had the beard, hair and sandals that used to be known as a 'Jesus' style, while his face and features looked uncannily archaic. It wasn't just that his clothes were a Nineties rendition of Sixties bohemia, his actual physiognomy seemed to come from thirty-five years ago. He looked like a Sixties revolutionary whose cause had just been irredeemably discredited; he wore a sullen scowl, and tried to make eye contact with everyone he brushed against.

Then, from even further back, there was a casually dressed couple in middle age; but her lemon trouser suit and his tan shoes made them look like the heroes of a cigarette advertisement, long since banned. On either side of them, a constant stream of shop assistants, temps and tourists. But today, I felt insecure in this montage of moods, and sought reassurance: where others find safety in numbers, I find safety in Selfridges. This department store seems synonomous with familiarity. Standing on its own rectangular island of city space, imperious and independent, the great inverted shoebox of Selfridges presents the weathered masonry of its Empire façade with a flourish which sings its own praises, reaching the crescendo, as it were, in the high solemnity of the welcoming angel who crowns the great clock above the ceremonial entrance.

The windows at street level look like the massive tanks of some giant aquarium. Today, lined and carpeted with reams of multicoloured crêpe paper, these tanks were each inhabited by three languid mannequins, female in form. They had the same shade and texture of whiteness as plaster of Paris or chalk dust. Tall and demure, their limbs tapering and elongated, they stood with one arm akimbo, hand on hip, and the other gesturing upwards, as though each extended open palm had once been carrying a tray of cocktails. Their bald white heads, with blank indentations to signify expressions of fashionable hauteur, were turned to the left and slightly inclined, deflecting the vulgarity of the stares they hoped for.

Each set of three mannequins had been dressed in the outfits of a different designer and their common theme was the promise of summer: linen suits, wraparound skirts, cotton dresses and snappy, athletic swimming costumes. And each window had a slogan: 'Love and Cool!', 'Wet and Wild!', 'Verve and Dash!' – panic and emptiness.

Like the office, this department store is a place of arcane geography; and, like the office, no matter how hard they try to introduce the urgency of a New Look – ceilings lowered, concessions reconfigured, walls removed – the tracery of its prehistory and founding atmosphere remains. There are still the battered, institutional side doors – such as you might have expected to find at the Science Museum twenty years ago – and the cavernous arena of the ground floor, with its scent like brown paper and mingled male colognes. Combined, all of the store's characteristics suggest constancy and security. I am not the first person to believe that nothing too bad can happen to you in a department store. Today, filled with that strange, nagging anxiety, I wandered through the perfume department in a mood of heightened receptivity. The various counters and displays, each declaring its *monde deluxe*, seemed like the thrilling, mysterious worlds which are conjoured up by the stage designs in an old-fashioned operetta.

(I felt as though I was looking down from the upper balcony of a theatre, into the clever reconstruction of a bohemian street scene. As the characters go their different ways, singing their farewells, the music softens to the dimming of the lights, and then the street is empty and enchanted by night. But the set designers have been clever enough to leave a lamp burning behind some shutters, even as a bell chimes midnight, and you are reminded of a childhood notion of night, at once supernatural and comforting, a place where the peacefulness of sleep is matched by the anticipation of secret, nocturnal presences.)

From the Perfume Hall, I made my way into the sombre world of men's socks and gloves. This is a space where you feel as though you are surrounded by collegiate panelling, and the dim light of cloisters. Idling through the aisles, I became engrossed in the various widths and weights of socks; I tried on a pair of string-backed driving gloves and tested their fit by making a fist and then splaying my fingers.

An assistant — a young woman, Middle Eastern perhaps — came up and asked if I needed any help. Her hair was so black it looked blue beneath the copper tone of the department's lighting. She was wearing a headband of green velvet. The dark blue suiting of her uniform — jacket and knee-length skirt — looked as though it was about to fall apart: the jacket had split just under one of the arms and the hem of the skirt had started to come down at the back. But there was nothing that the assistant could do to help me, even though my mood was feeling stranger by the minute. I was just looking.

She backed away and I clipped the gloves back on to their little hanger. I could smell the leather on my fingertips. I felt as though I had been out of the office for hours, but when I looked at my watch it was only ten minutes since I left North Row. The anxiety was still with me, but I began to realize that I could reduce the threatening immensity of its abstraction – panic and emptiness – to one specific apprehension: *it felt as though my life had reached critical mass*, and that there was simply no room in my being – myself as the embodiment of my consciousness – for any more lived experience.

And at this point I caught sight of Richard Hayter, who works along the corridor. Even from behind, I could recognize the shape of his head and the forceful bulk of his body. He was squatting on his haunches, fingering some garment that looked like a pair of swimming trunks. His jacket was stretched tightly across his shoulders, and his broad neck looked extremely pink and clean above the spotless whiteness of his shirt collar.

He was clearly deep in thought, pondering the ramifications of his purchase. Richard once told me, in the corridor, that the key to success was to eat an English breakfast, a Japanese lunch and a French dinner. He added, with some seriousness, that while such a diet was a sure route to advancement, he himself always avoided the cooked breakfast when he was attending a residential course or a conference away from town: 'You feel uncomfortable by mid-morning,' he explained.

Many years ago – although it still took me too long to work this out – I realized that it is always best to avoid your fellow employees should you catch sight of them out of the office. Otherwise, the self-consciousness will have set in almost as soon as your features have widened into the amiable countenance of a bland greeting. And this tends to be true, even on your good days. You should never dedicate those delicate moods of generosity which are born of inexplicable cheerfulness; such moods, in the office, contain vestiges of panic, and come across as odd, and, later, regrettable.

Also, you can wind up sounding like nothing more than a flatterer, and in the food chain of the office, as the different personalities maintain the eco-system by which they survive, the flatterer exists at a pretty low level, somewhere between the departmental sneak and the office clown.

It was for these reasons that I stopped in my tracks when I saw Richard Hayter. I just had time to notice that he was talking to himself, a whispered murmur of reasoning, as though he was trying to negotiate a difficult set of instructions. Pivoting on my heel, I turned down a parallel aisle. Now I was separated from my colleague by the height and width of a low counter, on my side of which there was a row of snow-white dinner shirts, and on his the tail-end of men's underwear. Making my way towards the shallow flight of steps which leads to the Food Hall, I got the impression that he had seen me.

I inhaled the aroma of the Food Hall: bread, cheese and coffee. I looked at the shellfish packed on ice. As usual, the displays of seafood were a spectacle. I stood with the rest of the mesmerized shoppers, staring down at the lobsters, crabs and oysters. We all wore a faintly suspicious expression, as though we were withholding judgement, but couldn't tear ourselves away.

In the Food Hall you can see the contours of other people's lives, or aspects of them at any rate. There were people ordering the food for whole dinner parties – Lebanese, English, Japanese; there were people buying themselves little treats – olives mixed with chillies, fresh anchovies and pasta. Elderly local ladies, with soft, powdered faces and their withered lips still carefully painted vermilion, were buying a few ounces of ham, or questioning the prices on jars of sweets or jam. You could see the impatience in the eyes of some of the young assistants, exasperated by having to wait for a customer to deliberate. And I imagined these ladies – another Old Guard, but unreconstructed this time as a modern idea – going back to their flats in Marylebone or Bayswater, and shaking their heads at the speed and the cost of it all.

Then I saw a sleek young couple who were both dressed in navy blue. She had lustrous black hair, a pale face, dark eyes that shone with self-assurance, and a wide, sensual mouth. She was wearing a bright red lipstick, the red of an Italian sports car. The tall man beside her, against whom she was constantly leaning, had a gentle, slightly startled expression, as though he found the transactions of simple shopping harmlessly confusing. Here was a couple, I thought, from Planet No Worries; they knew that they were free, and could be gently bewildered by everything forever. They had Made It. They had Won. I imagined that they were indulging their whims: a picnic of tomatoes and feta cheese, poppy-seed rolls and lobster mousse. (That's what they had in their basket.) I got the impression that they were having such a comfortable time, that it was almost unbearable to imagine their ease. *Dark eyes that shone, lobster mousse!*

I turned away, facing the floor-to-ceiling windows which look out on to Orchard Street. This is how the lunch hour goes. I saw that the clouds had moved on again, and the sun was making a summer's day in spring for the shoppers and the traffic. Just as I stepped out on to the street, I caught the perfume of lilies and cold water as it drifted from the florist's busy counter just to my left. That was the smell, I imagined, of an expensive hotel; as much as the smell of dusty carpet squares, spilled coffee and hot paper has always been the defining odour of the office.

Including the couple whom I had seen on Victoria Station earlier this morning, that sleek young couple dressed in navy blue were the second embodiment of pure glamour whom I had studied today. But as I walked towards the purchase of my lunchtime sandwich, I felt another of those sudden shifts in my habitual perception of the world. What made me so sure, that such good-looking, supposedly wealthy young couples were actually glamorous? And what exactly is glamour, anyway, and why does it enjoy such currency? I looked the word up once, in an etymological dictionary, and its roots are a conflation of 'language' and 'magic'. Clearly, the term has been abused – not least by yours truly over the years.

Kate, for instance, at the office, always looks too hungry to be glamorous; despite her tan and her perfect teeth she is ravenous for pleasure in a way which makes her anything but glamorous. Hence her monochromatic sense of values – ecstasy or petulance – which owns no tonal gradations of judgement. For Kate, the self-sufficiency of true glamour (although I have yet to define the term afresh) is denied by her dependence on circumstance to shape her moods. I could never imagine Kate looking anything other than jubilant or sulking. And yet there she is, known throughout North Row as 'Glamorous Kate'.

I suppose that I envy her the promise of prepared happiness which she always seems to possess with such nonchalance. She would never waste her lunch hour – or her life, come to that – on the thought that her experience of living could one day reach critical mass and fill her with a sense of panic and emptiness. And even as I was thinking that, I had the further sensation that today felt like the last day in my life when everything might be changed for the better.

For somewhere amidst my thoughts of Kate and glamour and all of the rest of it, I began to feel that I was running out of first days of the rest of my life. Why all of this had to happen on one particular day I can't tell you. But it was frightening. Perhaps what it meant was that – along with discarding my adolescent romance of becoming the urban anthropologist – it was time to accept that the promises of glamour, too, were only a mirage to keep you going. Like musicals during the Depression. And then what?

With her eye to invigilating the moods of young men, who fancied themselves perceptive, it's a wonder that Christine Kleenex never pointed out the constitution of glamour. Just a reminder, perhaps, that glamour draws its strength, like eroticism, from being forever beyond reach. We've all got our quotation from Shakespeare, just like we've all got our big relationship story, and mine is: 'My presence, like a robe pontifical, ne'er seen but wondered at' – advice on how to be a monarch.

Considering the subject from my point of view as a consumer, what seems to make a person glamorous is a sure-footedness of temperament: an inner, instinctive ability to bring together a configuration of traits, which articulates, above all, a monopoly on some state of independent, desirable orginality.

But the highest forms of glamour usually turn to squalor and eccentricity: having broken the sound barrier of personal development, as it were, glamour makes a person ethereal but still vulnerable to corporeality and the common business of living. Which is why all those film stars and celebrities turn out to have broken toilets and fridges filled with mouldy food — Bouviers living in a derelict beach house, Capote pissing on the stairs.

To be dandyfied, as a secret agent, an urban anthropologist or even an absentee from the office seeking the city, had always struck me as the fast track to glamour: to embody an attitude, a philosophy, in one's personal style. I must have spent years, in one way or another, burrowing through the commentaries on the theology of Style. And I came to the conclusion that Style can only be a means to an end; that if Style can articulate perception, then — what are you going to do with all those perceptions? Where do they go? Or do they just accumulate and reach critical mass? Whatever. My blood sugar level was low, and all my speculations gave way to the need for a sandwich.

People do all kinds of things in their lunch hour in order to get through the day, and you can find out a great deal about contemporary society by studying their habits. But George Crown, who does something in the Technical Services Department, and who wears a white suit to the office from May to September, has been getting drunk in his lunch hour for the last seven years. He manages to do this in a way which makes him seem puritanically censorious, rather than the red-nosed soak of popular mythology. Reeking of booze, he strides around the corridors in the afternoon glaring at anyone who is even carrying a cup of coffee. He finds fire hazards. He tries to mend the photocopying machine, even though it works quite properly.

I have spent my lunch hours looking for myself. Can you understand what I mean by that? My earliest recollection of lunch hour goes back to the City of London, when I was working at Waste. This was when I was new to the world of work, and each fresh experience, from the commuters crossing the bridge in the morning, to the gatherings in pubs in the early evenings, were entering my life as though through eyes which had been wired open. This was The Life; this was what most of us have to get on with.

On my very first lunch hour, just as I was hoping to escape on my own, free for sixty minutes from the need to appear attentive, grateful and friendly, a young man of my own age called Ron invited me to go with him to the staff canteen. His approach was so kindly that to refuse would have seemed offensive.

In those days, the staff canteens at the big City offices were more or less unchanged since the Fifties or even the Thirties. At our office, the canteen was in a kind of sub-basement, and reached by an echoing service corridor which was long and poorly lit. The floor of this corridor was covered in a highly polished linoleum which was the colour of raw steak. At one end, on the stroke of twelve noon, two vast white doors were unlocked and pushed back flat against the cold, green-painted brick of the walls. There was a strong smell of mince and custard.

Ron and myself joined the troop of workers – nearly all from the clerical levels, Post Room or Maintenance – who were making their way to an early lunch. It was a predominantly male crowd, too – 'the women all sit at their desks with an apple' said Ron (wrongly, as it turned out) – and here and there I saw elderly men with downcast eyes and utterly impassive faces whose solitude seemed surrounded by a dark and formidable moat of silence. Catching me eyeing one of these ancient clerks, Ron raised his eyebrows in an expression which mingled sympathy with criticism.

We queued to reach the stainless steel counter, which was lit and kept hot by a strip of dazzling, unshaded lights, hanging at eye level. I looked at the rows of plain wooden tables, each set with a glass jug of water and an ashtray. The women behind the counter were all West Indian. They patiently exchanged jokes with their regular customers, as they shovelled out slices of steak and kidney pie or piles of chips. These jokes were nearly all based on making do and getting by, but the kitchen workers would only agree with the chirpy one-liners; they were not complicit, for one minute, with any idea that we were all in the same boat.

I can't remember what I had to eat — the same as Ron, probably — but I had the impression that I was locked within an institution. The canteen made it clear that one was owned by the office, and it was hard to believe that beyond those cold, green walls and bowed male heads there existed a modern world of magazines, pop music and underground trains. But my kindly instructor clearly believed that lunch could be no more appetizing or convenient than this. And, certainly, it was convenient. The usual practice was to eat your lunch as quickly as possible and then have time to go to the pub. I bolted down my scalding food and then strode off behind my companion.

But Ron must have sensed that I hadn't enjoyed myself. We got back to the office at three minutes to one, having taken the early lunch; and I couldn't help noticing the faint expression of puzzled sadness in Ron's soft brown eyes, as he looked at me for just a few seconds longer than seemed natural when he left me back at my desk. And then I had the prospect of a long afternoon ahead of me, with indigestion and a burnt tongue.

Once again, it was all to do with being an audience or a performer: that problem which proves weakness. The following day, I made my excuses to Ron in advance; but even as I was babbling my lengthy explanation of how

I was forced to spend my lunch hour running urgent personal errands, I knew that I was creating a situation in which I was claiming to want nothing more than to make a whole routine of going to the office canteen. In my fear of being disliked, I felt as though I must surrender my autonomy so as not to risk displeasure. But why? What was it I feared?

Crossing Orchard Street today, with the sun warming the grey fabric of my suit, I found that these recollections of my earliest lunch hours were connected to the sense I had of my lived experience having reached critical mass: it was as though there wasn't room for any more memories. It occurred to me that this feeling of having reached the capacity of my days could be attributed to the fact that I had sealed, with resentment, bitterness or self-disgust, the vents through which I might have exhaled the breath of my true nature. That is, the nature of being out of step.

Surely, if I had given up my lunch hour all those years ago in Cannon Street so as not to offend Ron, then it was more than likely that I had given up whole portions of my freedom (I was going to say 'destiny') simply to keep in step with society itself? Of course, there was once a time when Paul and myself felt sure that the direct expression of our beliefs, made articulate through our lifestyle, was the banner beneath which to march. We lacked the essential courage perhaps. Or perhaps we just couldn't be bothered. After all, we trusted no one.

Today, when I think of the people who like to be seen as having turned against society, brandishing their plans for some ferret-faced Utopia or other, I can't help thinking that those stickers which you see beside the escalator on the tube – the 'Stop The City', 'Society Is Mentally Ill' brigade – are just as depressing as a boxed jigsaw turning brown in the window of a closed sub-post office. Paul and I declared 'If that's the alternative society, we'd sooner work in a bank'. And in a bank is exactly where we both ended up. In my case, donating my lunch hour to Ron Ryan's idea of a well-balanced day.

Ron wore a brown suit, with a faint chalk pinstripe; he was one of those young men who are very tall, with a pronounced Adam's apple and a cluster of firey pimples on the back of his neck, just above his slightly wash-rotted shirt collar. He had come to the bank straight from school, like so many of the clerks in Waste, and even though he was approaching his twenty-first birthday by the time that I met him, he still had the flushed awkwardness of adolescence: his hands, in particular, were long and red, with the fingernails bitten right down.

But still, twenty years later, I can bring Ron to mind as a representative of conscience. You had only to look at him – to see the way, for instance, he inwardly rejected the misanthropy of the older men who sat around us in the staff canteen, yet said nothing – to know that he was a decent type. He had a quality which marked him out as the clerical equivalent of the honourable schoolboy.

I thought, too, of how long ago it all seems. And yet I'm still a young man. I think that I use these memories like painters used to use a dark mirror — to readjust their eyes to the day's light.

Somewhere along Cannon Street, more or less facing the station, there was a low-fronted pub which served crusty rolls, filled with rubbery processed cheese and slices of watery tomato. With a bag of over-salted crisps, these rolls comprised my lunch for the best part of two years. The pub itself was remarkable in the fact that it had no atmosphere whatsoever; the place was as toneless as a waiting room. There were no shadowy nooks and crannies, no framed sepia photographs of Ludgate Circus in 1908, and not even the usual pub medley of fake panelling, blackboard menu and fruit machine.

All this pub had to offer was a carpet the colour of a stale green olive, and a few hard, straight-backed chairs. All the light came in from the front window, which looked out on the street with no attempt at decoration, curtaining, or even those stage props of Dickensian London — dusty port bottles and engraved caricatures of florid, Victorian barristers — which breweries must buy in bulk from some warehouse somewhere.

When I first went to Waste, the world of takeaway sandwiches was still a cold and benighted place, enduring its darkest hour before the dawn of new fillings. And how those fillings would stand for an epoch! On a par, perhaps, with the invention of oil paints.

Back then, most of the City sandwich bars were still run by large Italian familes who offered the hungry office worker a choice of ham, cheese salad, chicken or crabstick — with maybe some salami, or a slice of turkey, greying and greasy. Between the hours of twelve and two, these cafés would all present the same scene: behind the small counter, with its refrigerated display of sweating ingredients, you would find the entire family who owned and ran the place — and everyone with a job to do.

The fathers and sons would be leaning forward with tense, concentrated expressions, compiling the orders that were called out to them by the mother or one of her glamorous daughters. (For here was true glamour — language and magic.) The men would be working as though on a complex assembly line, flicking up slices of ham or spoonfuls of pickle with deft, repetitive gestures; every so often one of the sons would let out some quick comment — delivered with a sideways smile and in the opposite direction to his customer — which could lead you to guess that these boys really did think that most of their clients were a sorry bunch of losers. Only the father would remain obedient to the steady application of all of his faculties to the speedy delivery of freshly-made sandwiches.

Meanwhile, his wife and daughters — usually dark-haired but in one particularly crowded establishment off Cheapside, devastatingly blonde — would be handling the till and the coffee machine. They worked to the roar of steam, frothing the milk in polystyrene cups. The daughters, it seemed, were always kept just behind the firing line, away from the baleful or lustful stares of all the men who were waiting in the queue; the men with machine-coffee breath, dandruff on their collars, and those dull, thudding headaches which are brought on by a mixture of office lighting and the constipation caused by too many takeaway sandwiches.

Two centuries ago, these Italian daughters would have inspired those painters for whom sublime beauty could be found in feminine servility as a symbol of moral purity. Now, in their coffee-stained white shirts and short, black skirts, the allure of these young women was more that of forbidden virgins, even though they returned the stares which they received with glances that were blank with boredom.

These families toiled in the Dark Ages of the sandwich lunch. Some of them toil there still. But in the early years of the 1980s you could say that a long low band of light began to shine across the far horizon of this dark world; for a few minutes more, there was the stillness of pre-dawn, until finally the new sun arose, clarioned by the promise, *'So Much Of Everything'* – and to guarantee this promise, the birth of the sophisticated sandwich.

This afternoon, as I descended into the air-conditioned chill of the enormous Marks & Spencer Food Hall, on the corner of Orchard Street, W1, I realized that my sense of having reached my own critical mass of experience was mirrored by this broader notion that there is now so much of everything: sandwiches, technology, holidays, shoes, cars, records, TV channels, restaurants, you name it.

The teenage tourists whom I had just seen trailing down Oxford Street, each with their little haversack dangling between their shoulder blades, had grown up surrounded by so much of everything. But they were also aware of those who have nothing: the ones who are always on the News, with their civil wars and their famines.

This is the unbelievable Fuck Up. We all know about the unbelievable Fuck Up and we are nearly all in constant denial about it. It's just the Fuck Up. And we have arranged our thinking so that none of us is actually accountable for it.

So today, in the hall of So Much Of Everything — which is as white and brightly lit as any gallery of modern art — I chose a deep-filled, low-fat tuna and sweetcorn sandwich on wholemeal roasted onion bread, and a carton of mango and apple juice, and a kind of biscuity thing made out of honey and oats.

There was quite a long queue and I was standing behind a woman who was buying three raspberry pavlovas and four bottles of Buck's Fizz, for a leaving party by the looks of it. But all the time I was waiting, the oddness of the day grew more insistent: panic and emptiness, critical mass, dark eyes and lobster mousse, so much of everything . . . I closed my eyes and felt my lashes grazing against one another. The air in the office dries out my eyes and I measure out my life with Optrex.

You can leave the Food Hall by an escalator which takes you up to street level. During the brief ascent, you leave behind the cold scent of fresh fruit and plastic bags (the fragrance of thermo-destabilized convenience snacks) and enter the warm pungency of woollens. Stepping off the escalator, I made my way between racks and racks of skirts and trousers and cardigans. I looked up towards the big photographs – made up of nine connected panels, in three rows of three – which depict two young women with tanned bodies and welcoming expressions, relaxing in white underwear: the deep-filled sandwich made flesh. All over Europe, men would be looking at these examples of a monolithic, domestic pornography – *so much of everything!* – as they carried their bottles of Buck's Fizz and their raspberry pavlovas and their bagged bistro-style salad back to the office in their lifestyle lives.

Outside, the sun was still shining. The corner of Orchard Street was crowded with ranks of people, looking severe as they waited to cross the road. Quite a few of them were wearing sunglasses. Ahead of me, two teenage girls with healthy, bobbed hair, dressed in baggy canvas trousers and singlets of Army green, were surveying these crowds with pensive expressions. They too, were each wearing a pink rucksack which hung between their shoulder blades. I could see the pink nylon webbing of the straps beginning to cut into their shoulders. They had probably walked from one of the big hotels in Paddington; the beds would still be unmade in their sparse, airless room, and their digital travel clock would be flicking off the seconds of early afternoon on the shabby bedside cabinet.

There is probably some molecular chain of phenomena, with each molecule, so to speak, triggering the next, which connects the pink nylon webbing of those biting rucksack straps to the incineration of surplus food dumps and the dereliction of farms in central Africa; to the heat of sand and rocks against bare feet, and the opening up, before someone's exhausted eyes, of a limitless tract of parched land.

In the midst of the unbelievable Fuck Up − the Fuck Up of such epic proportions that you can barely see it (like one of those buildings which are so big that you can only see them from the air) − there are choices to be made that we all try to dodge. I remembered Paul waiting on the steps of Saint Paul's to lend me some money years ago. It was a wet spring day. He was wearing his long raincoat. I saw him pacing along the top of the steps, holding his cigarette at chest height in a pose of unselfconscious elegance.

This memory came back to me as I turned down Lumley Street and walked the last few steps to North Row. We must have been so young when we made the choices which shaped us, and then denied that we had a choice, in the midst of the Fuck Up and so much of everything.

But then I knew, as I carried my sandwiches back into the office, that choices are a blessing in a world where choice is so often denied – and that I have a choice. And then the thought slipped away again, like a fish darting into the darkness of reeds.

SIX

'. . . an object of social usefulness.'

I walked straight into this ending of a sentence, as though it had been lying in wait for me. Delivered like a punchline, in the suave, ironical tone which deadpan comedians use when they're backing up a gag with a wide-eyed appeal for support, the trigger of this *aperçu* fired a burst of delighted laughter. But I couldn't see the speaker even as I heard his words entertaining the other half of the office.

I sat down at my desk and saw the Systems Amendment forms which I had been shuffling around earlier in the morning. They were, of course, exactly as I had left them: a pell-mell mess of printed sheets – some white, some pink, some blue. I had forgotten all about them during the morning meeting and the lunch hour, and, confronted by their stubborn presence, I felt that sudden weight of sullen depression which follows a reminder of our powerlessness in the face of certain situations.

I opened my packet of sandwiches and stuck the straw into my carton of juice. It is always a risk, eating your sandwiches at your desk when you've already used up your lunch hour; but there is also the chance that you might look as though you are working straight through your lunch hour and simply grazing as you work. At a certain level in the office, you are guilty until proven innocent. The executive assumption of the New Professionalism — that everyone is totally dedicated to their work, all of the time — has not extended to include me.

Today, eating my tuna sandwich in a series of mechanical bites, I had the sensation that if I didn't seize, somehow, on the feelings that these strange moods were arousing in me, then I would miss some vital event in my life. The idea that in the midst of everything, choice exists.

Paul once calculated that a man in his office would have eaten a tuna sandwich the size of a small car in the time that he had known him, working on the basis of a tuna sandwich every day, five days a week, for so many years, etc, etc.

None of my assistants was at their desks. Through the window on the other side of the room, I could see a small patch of shadow sliding across the side of a building as a cloud passed under the sun. The air seemed softer, just looking at it. I carried on munching away, to the accompaniment of indistinct voices and a sudden, explosive guffaw. That could only be Mike Catherall. This noise was coming from the half of the office that was hidden from view. I wish I could explain how drawn

I felt to the warming day outside, but I can only describe what I saw through the window — buildings in the sun — as kindness. *The kindness of unimpeachable honesty.*

There was another roar of laughter from the carnival gathering around the corner. It felt as though there was a party being held in our two rooms, but that everyone except me had drifted into the other room, drawn together by their shared opinions and expectations, and that singularity of purpose which was keeping the whole thing afloat.

Years ago, in dark suburban sitting rooms, where all the other teenagers looked tanned and lovely by the crimson glow of the low party lights, I discovered my ability to generate indifference. At Sunsan Henshaw's seventeenth birthday party, for instance. Christine Kleenex said that it was the loners at parties who most wanted to join in the fun. How romantic those suburban villa gardens seemed, filled with magnolia blossom, luminous in the dusk. Girls I had never seen before, slim and flippant, would be deep in breathless conversations which I always imagined were planning the attainment of some giddy private pleasure — the summit, the peak!

By now it was getting on for half past two. Perry appeared, owlish and jocular, from the other side of the baize partition. He sat down at his desk with the expression of a person who has dined well on merriment. Leaning back in his chair, he called out 'Exactly!' to a person whom I couldn't see. Then he looked over and asked if I knew when Frankie and Irene's leaving party was due to start.

We chatted for a few minutes and I noticed that we were both accent hopping. Accent hopping is a reflex which occurs in the office when you quite simply alter your accent to suit the person you're talking to. Well-bred clerks will start trying to speak like real life Cockneys in certain situations, and then will revert to their natural dialect as soon as their boss walks in. Perry, having been verging on East London exclamations in the other half of the office, was now talking to me as though I was his doctor. Then again, to repay his intimacy, I was talking back in a tone that was suddenly jaunty.

In a confusion of pointless but friendly laughter, we agreed that we had both better turn up at Frankie and Irene's leaving party. Then Perry's phone rang, and Anne walked in, clutching a sheaf of papers.

'I keep forgetting about those bloody crates.' She emphasized the gesture of breathing in as she squeezed around them.

'We've just been talking about all the things we ought to leave behind,' said Perry, his big hand cupped over the phone, 'And the people we ought to leave behind as well.' He looked down at his desk as he returned to his call, but it seemed to me that he had thrown a glance in Anne's direction. Some kind of joke that I wasn't supposed to notice. '. . . an object of social usefulness . . .': the phrase came back to mind, and made me feel sad. The peak and the summit had always been a hill too far away. I imagined a girl's dark bedroom in the suburbs, as it might have been years ago, before she got married. A peacock feather in an empty mineral water bottle; a record collection; a dully flickering filament of scarlet light.

Then Dave came striding back into the room, bursting with a public display of energy. He was wearing his most serious expression, which is to say that he wanted everyone to know that he was annoyed about something. When he gets into this mood, a small cleft appears, like a dent, in the tip of his nose. His jacket was off, and the sleeves of his pale blue shirt were rolled up to the elbow.

There is a particular style which Dave puts across. It is a kind of transatlantic slickness but the effect is strangely effete. This afternoon, for instance, the way he had folded back the double cuffs of his shirt, allowing for his square, gold cuff-links to dangle free like foppish insignia, was matched by the fact that the grey woollen fabric of his trousers seemed to be stretched just a little too taut across his neat behind. The overall image is snug, in a way which seems too pleased with itself.

'I thought you'd gone to lunch?' said Perry.

Dave just muttered something and sat down at his desk. Then he looked at the blue removal crates and pulled a face. He too had forgotten all about them during the lunch hour. 'Great,' he said.

'Isn't it funny how we all had that big meeting this morning, about the move, and then you get on with something else and keep forgetting about it?' This was Anne.

'We've got to call it a "migration", not a move,' said Perry. His own belongings – a few files, some folders – were already packed. 'Sick Building Syndrome is when you get too many positive ions, isn't it?' he continued, speaking as though from the heart of some private calculation, for which he needed a few more facts to reach the right answer.

'It isn't Sick Building,' said Anne. 'It was Sick Building before they did the refit; now it's just . . .'

'What's up with you?' Perry was ignoring Anne and staring at Dave, who was banging the drawers of his desk shut as he pulled out folders filled with loose papers.

'Tell you later.'

Dave's tone was brusque, but it conferred the status of trusted confidant on Perry, who acquires his sense of masculinity, vicariously, from his male colleagues.

'But then it was asbestos, which was worse.' Anne was now speaking to the office in general; and I told her how I could remember the contractors making corridors within corridors out of some kind of air-tight blue sheeting, and how there were all these men wandering around in what look liked space suits, while people were still sitting at their desks, oblivious to the whole thing, without so much as a hanky over their mouths. I must have tickled

Anne's funny bone, because when I'd finished the story – I speak rather quietly – she immediately turned to Perry and Dave and said, 'Did you hear that? They built –'

Just then Kate arrived. Glamorous Kate. But a glance was enough to see that something was wrong. She walked quickly towards her desk with her head lowered. Her face was flushed and her eyes slightly red. She wiped her nose with a screwed-up rag of tissue. Dave looked up at her and then continued to pull things out of his desk drawers, more or less tossing them into one of the crates. Layer after layer of office detritus was divided between the bin and the crates, including a page torn out of a pornographic magazine and a paper knife with a bone handle, which Perry said he would have if Dave didn't want it. Anne, for her part, was trying to find an expression which combined sisterly concern towards Kate with respect for another person's privacy; the result was that she kept biting her lower lip. Needless to say, the atmosphere in the office had become tense and awkward.

Statistically, four-thirty in the afternoon on Tuesdays is the time when people feel at their lowest spirits in an office. Today, I seemed to hit that rock of my own accord, two hours early and on the wrong day. Having felt such shifts in my moods, and those moments of heightened sensitivity, having seen the light outside as kindness, I now felt my ancient resentments coming back.

The truth of the matter (I said to myself) is that my boss hates me and my colleagues just think I'm ridiculous. Well, perhaps 'hate' is too strong a word to describe Potter's feelings towards me. His irritation with my failure has simply turned into the beginnings of a personal dislike. And the worst thing is, I don't blame him. To be honest with you, I think that the whole situation has got out of hand. And this afternoon I was torn between the longing to resign and a terror of redundancy – 'nowhere to go but indoors', as I quoted at the beginning. But I need the money.

But it wasn't always like this. When they first took me on, here at North Row, they told me they were pleased to have me on board. Potter himself used to take me aside for little confidential chats about some aspect of the office, and talk with me as though to an equal – lowering his voice if ever anyone else came within earshot, and wishing me a good weekend when he popped his head around the door on Friday evenings.

I found this attention embarrassing and flattering, all at the same time. It did make me want to work hard for the company, but something just seemed to go wrong. I was always afraid of saying the wrong thing, and I would sometimes walk away from those little conversations with white semi-circles in the palms of my hands, where I had been digging my nails into them. This was back in the old days, before the grey carpets and the Four Assistants of the Apocalypse.

So what went wrong? Because however much I might want to blame the office for my boredom, bitterness and lack of promotion, I know in my heart – or I have discovered in my heart, today – that a part of myself must have wanted to turn out like this. For a long time, I have been telling myself that people like me just can't make a success of office life. But why?

It is partly to do with being out of step; but then there is something else, some quality which just makes us difficult to like, and which keeps us off the loop of professional cleanliness. Perry, for instance, is always described as 'easy going' and 'a good bloke'. Perhaps, in the end, it's down to your ability to join in. People who can't join in are like those people whose surnames could just never become famous, no matter how many operas their bearers wrote.

In the past I have believed that what went wrong was the usual decline spiral which can bring down any office career: boredom leads to neglect of duties, which leads to mistakes, which leads to censure, which leads to lack of confidence, which leads to more mistakes, more censure, lack of motivation and more boredom. Like the economy of a town going bust and then the crime rate goes up.

But on my second day at North Row I was so eager to shine. The beardless neophyte, marching to work. I was entrusted with twelve large ledgers, which were filled with sheets of finely ruled paper, covered with tiny columns of figures. These days, of course, it's all done on computers; but my first job was to monitor the totals of these figures, and to coerce, if you want, a meaning from them. I was a One-Man Waste, without the spectacle of Les's bull-fighter approach to finding the dropped figures in a running total. These ledgers were called 'the Stats'. There was a shelf behind my first desk at North Row where they were kept. To be more precise, the Stats had to be continually updated from diaphanous slips of paper – sometimes solitary and elegaic, on other occasions in great bundles – which would arrive in circulation envelopes with my name upon them. And it was the sight of my name on these envelopes which used to amaze me. I found it so hard to believe that I had conducted my life in such a way as to arrive behind this desk, personally responsible for the lumpen contents of these brown envelopes. Time and again I would ask myself, 'How did this happen?'

At the beginning, I tried to square up to my task. I kept my own personal record (unasked) of all the adjustments to the Stats which I had entered into the files themselves. Potter found out about this and announced the innovation at the weekly staff meeting. Which was kind of him, I suppose, but I had built my own gallows. In the first place, the old hands in the office thought that I was making them look lazy, which they resented. And in the second place, I quickly discovered that it would take me all day to maintain my two records of Stat amendments, the one official, the other auxillary, and so I let my own records lapse.

Then, of course, Potter asked to see them. Discovering

that I had given up my new system, his expression as he looked in my little book — like a man reading the last diary entries of a marooned sailor who had gone mad from drinking sea water — went from concern to sorrow. And things were never the same again between us. The Stats expanded, to become 'Systems', and I'm on Systems Amendments. Incidentally, those little slips of paper were called 'the deads'. I've just remembered that.

I don't have to work hard to retrieve my memories of the office; it is as though every office I have ever worked in is always around me, as a landscape, and I see them whenever I look up from my desk.

Today, this landscape seemed to stretch as far as the eye can see, and I felt that I knew every inch of it, because it is also my accumulated experience: the valleys of dwindling ambition drop down from the mountains of hope, and on the valley floors you will find that the paddy fields of resentment are watered by the streams of wasted time. I could paint you a picture, in the classical allegorical style, which would depict the whole thing. But I would be sure to show this landscape in a warm, amber light: the low winter sun of the Compensatory Pleasures.

As anyone who works in an office will tell you — they won't, actually — the Compensatory Pleasures are what keep the whole thing going. Not just the office, but the whole thing. The Compensatory Pleasures are pretty much self-explanatory: they are all the rewards, big and small, which we give to ourselves to keep us going. They tend to be addictive. Their existence, and our dependence upon them, fuels the consumer economy, capitalism, society and so forth. They are the little treats and habits which we develop to compensate for some quality that we feel is either lacking or stolen from our lives. Simultaneously, therefore, they are the anaesthetics to soothe resentment. And the more one works in resentment, the greater the need for the Compensatory Pleasures.

Over the years of working days in London, I have seen many different forms of Compensatory Pleasure. Once you start thinking about them, they tend to crowd your vision. You might tend to think of the sharper end of their allure: the alcohol and sex for sale which can tempt the resentful office worker on his way to Victoria or Charing Cross. But those economies are less important, as Compensatory Pleasures, than the more subtle versions – from having to walk the same route, every day, to discovering that certain habits have become necessities. The Compensatory Pleasures also tend to obscure your view of what you really want from your life: they're the short-term, instant gratification hit. On the senior Training Courses, these days, they use a lot of Neuro-Linguistic Programming – a kind of mind-wash, based on positive thinking – and at the heart of that technique lies the question, 'What do you want?'

The Compensatory Pleasures will give you a lot of false answers to that question, posing as truths, but they keep the whole caboodle going, from Starter Home to Pension Plan. They can be made healthy, I suppose, but that would require a bringing to consciousness of the whole thing — So Much of Everything and the Unbelievable Fuck Up. Perhaps you reach that consciousness through panic and emptiness.

I was thinking this, and had just finished separating the white Systems sheets, when I noticed, stuck at a vicious angle to the screen of my computer monitor (which was the same dank green as a stagnant millpond, as usual) a primrose yellow post-it note with two words and two initials scrawled upon it: 'See me. B P'.

'Oh, he left that just after you'd gone to lunch,' said Anne, who had been watching me. I made the usual 'wonder what that's all about then?' grimace and wandered off down the corridor to get on with the photocopying. The ancient art of photocopying has fallen into some neglect, since we all signed up to the marching cohorts of Information Technology. In this much, it resembles the fate of correction fluid — which seldom shows up these days in the slim, glossy brochures of office stationery, and must seem prehistoric to the slim, glossy assistant who actually orders the stationery.

It isn't that I am resistant towards new technology: I just can't be bothered with all of the obeisance and genuflection with which it is worshipped. It should be added, I think, that this is another male aspect of the office, at root. All those rams, and hard drives and bytes and rebooters. I annoyed the men downstairs by calling our system Quirky Wordspurt.

On the subject of names, I have noticed that there is a particular type of patrician female office worker, usually in their late twenties, who all have names which sound as though they came from a gynaecological dictionary. Self-assured, with flawless skin, their names sound like Vulva, Vagina, Clitoris and Labia. You can imagine them answering the phone, with 'Vulva's not here at the moment,' or, 'I'm sorry, Clitoris is away from her desk; it's Vagina, can I take a message?'

Not that women of this type work at North Row. We have a great many Nathalies and Traceys — all the names ending in 'y' and 'ie' — who must be a kind of female serfdom to the 'a' and 'is' names of the gynaecological register of posh girls who work.

The photocopier is kept in a windowless space between two sets of fire doors, one of which was propped open with a fire extinguisher when I arrived this afternoon with my sheets. I like this area, with its pale grey walls, and its strong scent of clean, modern chemicals. The light is diffused as though under water. As a space, this area hasn't deserved a framed print, but there is a glass box screwed to the wall, framed in scarlet metal, with a little steel hammer attached to it by a delicate chain. Whenever I stand here, watching the flat white light of the photocopier slide to and fro with a hum and a bump, I think of the phrase 'form and function'.

Today, this phrase was suddenly melded into the sound of a woman's voice saying 'fucking'. At first I thought I must have imagined it. As I was thinking 'form and function', she had said 'fucking'? It didn't seem likely. I frowned, and then heard another woman saying, in an urgent, ecstatic whisper, hissing with giggles, 'Sshh . . .!' And then there was another clunk, as another Systems Amendment form (white) was copied, and its copy slid gracefully into the collection tray. The two women's voices had stopped, and although I couldn't actually see who was speaking – they were just inside the door of the adjoining office – I could tell that one of them was trying to hold her breath so as not to burst out laughing.

Then, just as I was straightening my next original – I can never find the A4 demarcation lines by instinct, like some people – one of the women put her head around the door, rather in the manner of Charlie Chaplin peering around a tenement wall to see if the fat policeman has moved on. I didn't know the woman's name, but I recognized her as one of Anne's friends: part of a clique which has earned itself the title 'Hot Gossip'. A little under forty, at a guess, this woman has a heavy, lampshade fringe and her hair is on the orange side of auburn. She wears a lot of mascara and describes herself at office parties as a right little raver.

I also happen to know that her bathroom suite is in a shade called 'Peach Whisper' because I overheard her talking about it one day as I was walking down the corridor. And she has a friend who inherited a pub in west London, somewhere near Kensal Road.

Having stared at me for about ten seconds, with a look which mingled suspicion with indignation, she seemed to suddenly recognize me as a person of no possible consequence. She raised her chin slightly as I finally allowed myself to return her look, and then she withdrew her head and returned to her unseen colleague. I seem to be one of those people whom nobody would regard as a threat. Sometimes, when I catch the adjudicating glance of a fellow worker, breaking off his anecdote as I walk into the room, I feel as though I must look like a deaf and dumb henchman in a spy story. I'd be wearing a dusty black suit, and be called Block.

This was the case at the photocopying machine this afternoon. But rather than trying to temper her story in the name of discretion, Lampshade Fringe seemed to revel in the details. She even looked to see if I was still listening, as the hot news of the lunch hour burned the very air around us with its particularly spicy contents. And I knew, almost before she carried on speaking, that this story was going to involve my assistant, Kate. Within these dry corridors, gossip of this kind spreads like bushfire; and, like bushfires, the causes of such gossip tend to have been smouldering away for quite a while – just beneath the surface of common knowledge – before finally catching a gust of publicity and bursting into flames. Such is the nature of office affairs.

Simon and Kate, it transpired, had just been reported to the Reception and Security desk by a telephone call from one Mr Kanova. Mr Kanova turned out to be our mysterious neighbour in the block of flats which face the office; to be more precise, he is the one whom rumour claims has a nanotechnological laboratory on a microchip implanted in his pineal gland. Kevin Waters has gone so far as to say that this chip has been installed by the aliens in such a way that any attempt to remove it would kill its host.

But any reports beamed back to the aliens from Mr Kanova's chip this afternoon would probably have included a fairly detailed description of human sexual behaviour. It seemed strange to me that Kate and Simon had chosen the roof for their rendezvous – unless, on a subconscious level, they wanted to be caught, and their relationship made public. Grinch, after all, is married with three children.

Hot Gossip were discussing the details of the case, accent-hopping to a tone of voice which asserted the maturity to be as graphic as it cared.

'. . . so he's leaning against the actual, you know, thing that goes around . . .'

'With her?'

'Well, all I know . . .'

I tuned out of their conversation and calculated that I was probably walking though Marks & Spencer just as Kate and Simon were giving way to their better judgements. I imagined Dave writing a letter to one of his magazines describing the event: 'There's some fantastic looking birds in the office where I work, and one of them . . .' But this doesn't suit Kate's personality, however much it might have suited the fetishised Kate who has been constructed within the ecstatic frustation of office lust. I thought how vile this must all be for Kate: the hyenas had finally brought down the antelope: Gotcha!

'But the roof!' This was Lampshade, luxuriating in incredulity.

'Well I say they're old enough and daft enough. It's not as though . . .'

'And poor old George had to go up there and tell them to knock it off! I'm surprised the climb didn't kill him, let alone the shock . . .'

Occasions such as these are pretty common. But would this story, I wondered, be suppressed and then buried, to join the Most Secret archive in North Row's forbidden library of office gossip? Or would it become brightly coloured and sedimentary, following the currents of rumour from office to office? It would join the story about the couple who screwed on Potter's desk, and the threesome who were supposedly found in the basement. These legends become a part of the compensatory pleasures, rolled over in the minds of the male employees, at least, as part of the secret life of work. And Mr Kanova has sent his transmission.

The office affair is as much a part of the office furniture as the three-drawer filing cabinet and the typist's orthopaedic chair. Collating my photocopied sheets in the order of their SAM numbers, I wondered how Kate and Simon would adjust to their new reputation. It would just be another part — a tiny, barely significant sub-strand — of the Unbelievable Fuck Up. Dave, on the other hand, is fairly proprietorial about his female equivalent, and Irene and Frankie's leaving party could yet turn into a grand opera, in which the arias are stared, rather than sung.

There are pubs to the east of Fitzrovia, obscure, lonely little pubs, tucked into the blocks between Cleveland Street and Gower Street, where the office affairs of the West End tend to hide out during the lunch hour. French kisses in the shadow of the Middlesex Hospital's Department of Toxicology. But I had no more room for any new memories, caught up as I was this afternoon with larger questions of destiny.

I knew that something was wrong as soon as I stepped back into the office. It seemed as though everyone was staring at me. And this was because everyone *was* staring at me, except Kate, who was leaning over some papers on her desk and not making eye contact with anyone. In the middle of the room, about half of the blue crates were filled with files and stationery. To be honest with you, the place looked a mess.

The other thing I noticed was that the office seemed far more crowded than usual; it was as though everyone at North Row who knew me was in the room. I assumed that this temporary hush was due to Kate's return from her overseen tryst on the roof, and that all of the people who appeared to be popping in and out of our office, or just standing around at the end of the room, had come along to rubberneck for smudged mascara and sudden resignations.

This may well have been the case. I never found out for sure, because it was at this point, just as I was strolling back to my desk, that two things happened to jolt my day yet again. Firstly, I suddenly found myself looking down at Anne; she appeared extremely scared, and she was trying to say something to me without being overheard, something urgent. But why was her face at a level with my desk? I had to lean down to try and hear what she was saying, in her hoarse whisper, filled with panic. I liked to think that my answering expression was one of friendly concern, but now I know that my face must have seemed the face of a fool.

I know this, because no sooner had I given kind-natured Anne a nod of encouragement to coax her to speak a little louder than I was shaken by a sudden bang, and the sound of words being fired at me in a voice which was cold, clipped and barely containing its anger. That's what I remember most: that Potter's anger was targeted directly at the very core of my being, the part which had reached critical mass, if you want.

I have very little experience of anger, having avoided other people's, for the most part, and ingested my own by turning it into depression or resentment. Hence my fear of that anger mutating into the alien of concealed illness. But this afternoon, in front of nearly everyone at North Row who knows me, Potter finally let loose his fury at my performance over the last few years. In this much, the ritual of humiliation had the same audience as a leaving party.

Potter's face had turned red and his eyes were fixed on mine, as though he was trying to bring me to my knees with the sheer weight of his disgust. The detonating charge had been some bit of lost paperwork; but this bit of lost paperwork, to Potter, had become a symbol of my contempt for the office, and, by extension, of my personal contempt for him.

'Just can't be relied upon to . . .'

Now came the forbidden statements: the words that you aren't supposed to speak in public. This was why the crowds had gathered, drawn by the tumbrils of the hanging judge.

'It is your responsibility to ensure that these files are

kept in order. What do you think Dave and Perry and
. . . Anne spend their time doing? Eh? Do you think
they've got the time to be sorting out your messes?
Well, do you? They're too busy to go around checking
that simple tasks are being done. You're supposed to be
a Team Leader for Christ's sake . . . And what about
the SAMs? Where are those?'

I handed him my photocopied sheets, and he flipped
through them without looking at them. He was rehearsing his next line.

'Useless.'

He threw the papers back on to my desk and began
to rummage through all the other paperwork. Then
he stopped, and looked at me. 'Well?' But I couldn't
think of anything to say. My expression, unfortunately,
must have looked a lot like a shrug. The quiet room
had become silent. Or perhaps, in the far distance, I
could hear someone starting a telephone call in neat,
business-like phrases which were squeaky clean with
virtue. I alone was reeking.

And then I remembered that Paul had once told
me: *the route to enlightenment is only reached when you
have been humiliated in front of the tribe*. The ego must
be broken down. And with that thought, my mounting
anger began to subside, and my whole body was filled
with the most delicious experience of inner peace. I had
been thinking about the uses of uncontrollable anger in
a controlled space; in other words, I had been seriously

considering picking up the heavy metal stapler (it's the size and weight of a steel ingot) and hitting Potter around the side of the head with it. You'll think that this is just bravado after the event, but I had actually felt my hand moving towards this blunt object.

And so I said nothing, but looked beyond Potter, and then blinked. I couldn't really blame him for his loss of patience; it was just so obvious that everything had gone sour in our dealings with each other, and that something had to change. But what? He turned away from me, and walked towards the door. His head was lowered, as though he was deep in thought.

Very gently I sat down at my desk and looked around the room. Dave was brooding. Perry was chattering into his phone, as usual, and Kate had clearly left her body. Now that it was open season on the blonde with the tan, she was left in an undefended situation. She could either make a joke of the whole thing, and be thought of as racy, or try to defend her dignity with silence. For both of us it was still too early to know if the equations of reputation would solve themselves.

'He's been in a mood all day,' said Anne.

'So have I.'

She gave me a little smile when I said this; and as she did I almost began to panic at how distant I felt from my surroundings. If Kate, too, had left her body in the wake of trauma, then there seemed to be every possibility that the two of us would meet somewhere over the rooftops, like Chagall's lovers in Room 404.

The crowds who had witnessed the launch of Potter's Rocket had now dispersed, and I had the feeling that my place down the food chain of office personalities had simply been confirmed by the public humiliation of being dressed down by a man who is probably no more than five years older than myself. I tried to think whether or not I hated Potter, or whether I hated the people who had stopped to watch his display of temper. Of course, my instinct was to try and feel superior to the office; these were the last vestiges of grandiosity, which my ritual humiliation in front of the tribe would soon disperse. And then I remembered Charlie Smith.

With a name like that, you imagine some carrot-top Cockney with a fund of wit and wisdom from the University of Life. But Charlie Smith wasn't like that at all. You can learn a lot about Charlie's story from the fact that he always referred to himself as Charles. He was friendly enough, but aloof, and he spoke in what now would be taken as a virtual parody of an upper-class English accent. But apparently his background — he was in his early sixties when he was retired from North Row — was working class, somewhere in the Midlands.

Self-taught and self-reconstructed as an urbane, world-weary aesthete, Charlie Smith was extremely cultivated and even the managers used to speak to him with great respect. And then one day I realized that they were simply humouring him. He was an old-fashioned clerk, and he had never really wanted to ascend from his clerkdom. He even described himself as 'a modernist extension of a Dickensian character'.

In the mornings, he would brew his own little pot of Lapsang Souchong and the area around his little desk would be filled with its smoky fragrance. He quoted poetry in a theatrical, declamatory voice, whenever he wanted to poke fun at some event in office politics. 'The Assyrian came down like the wolf on the fold' – when some suit could be seen marching towards another suit's desk; or 'Home they bore their warrior dead' when the same suit returned, downcast, from a less than successful meeting. A bachelor, Charlie Smith had surrounded himself with culture to keep the office at bay.

Needless to say, he didn't survive the grey carpets. He was lowered, slowly but surely, into a darker and darker place. He was teased by this process, in a gentle but persistent manner, and became a funny character within the office, a kind of tourist attraction, more oddity than mascot.

(At the same time, there was a statuesque, blonde young woman who was perhaps in her middle twenties, and who worked on the sixth floor. She looked like an erotic cartoon of a sexy girl. She wore tight skirts, high heels, clinging tops and bright lipstick. And the office's way to deal with her, too, was to treat her like a mascot. In fact, Charlie Smith could have been Arthur Miller to her Marilyn Monroe. Except for the fact that she left to marry a professional landscape gardener.)

But when Charlie left he gave a little speech, and, sitting at my desk this afternoon feeling so peculiar, I remembered his closing words: 'But I want to say something to you young people, and that is this: remember, They haven't got a sense of humour.' And then there was a bit of uneasy shuffling at the back of the leaving party, as the management weathered this last little squall with a few exchanged glances and eyes raised to Heaven.

Back in those days, they used to hold leaving parties in the chilly basement of North Row, a vast, curiously shaped place which smelt of floor polish and insulated wires. This basement – where the threesome was supposedly discovered – had at one time been fitted out as a function room. There was a long, narrow serving hatch, which was now shuttered and locked, which looked out from a kind of small bar. In the corner of this bar there was a tiny stainless steel sink; but neither of the taps worked anymore, and the basin was covered in a dried, cement-coloured powder which was some sort of cleaning stuff, hardened with age. Also, there were two equally dry shower cubicles, which looked like the scene of a murder, or the set of a hard core video.

For a while, they kept a vending machine down in

this basement. It was placed against the far wall, and as the basement was always in semi-twilight, owing to the low wattage of the few strip lights which had been left to flicker, you could see the illuminated panels of this machine glowing across the room at you, for all the world like a captive robot which you had crept downstairs to liberate.

During the vending machine years in the basement's melancholy history, I used to go down there sometimes and try to relate the past of this room to its present atmosphere. It had the feel of a buried dynasty, because it dated back to a time before our company leased this building. In this much it seemed bereft. I even tried to sleep one afternoon in one of its murky corners but I found it too depressing.

Charlie Smith's leaving party was the last to be held in the basement. He got his Black Forest gateau, his boxed set of Janet Baker singing Mahler and his chance to say a few words, all in the dim yellow light of the basement beneath a pavement in the West End of London.

Today's party, for Frankie and Irene, would be in the modern style. We live in an increasingly secular society, after all.

SEVEN

Just after five this afternoon, most of the blue crates in the middle of our office were nearly full. The room looked much bigger somehow. Also, I saw my own desk as though for the first time. As Dave and Anne were tying up their bundles of current paperwork with pink fabric ribbon, I found myself looking at my desk and realizing that it was a good deal older and smaller than any of the others. How could I never have noticed that before? And I felt a sudden rush of sentiment for this poor, shabby little desk, as though it was an old and overworked donkey which was standing patiently in the corner of a field.

As I began to empty the drawers, I found stationery and paperwork which dated back nearly a decade. It is a bad offence of mine that whenever I find myself confronted with a piece of work which is simply too difficult, boring or awkward to be dealt with easily, I put it at the back of a drawer and more or less will it into the Realm of Unbeing. Thus, at the back of my desk drawers today, I found a concertinaed wedge of papers, many of which had Respond By dockets that had been stapled into place by people who have long since retired.

These were the sins which could never be confessed: the evidence of a botched career and the cause – if not the explanation – of a life in the slow lane. Here was another of those molecular chains of phenomena – like the one which connects the pink nylon rucksack straps to the derelict farm in central Africa – which held in its very smallness the immensity of wasted years. All I could think of doing was stuffing the whole lot into a bin liner and hope that nobody would notice. I had to turn my back while I was doing this, because Anne, in particular, would be more than likely to point out that I was throwing away my work.

But what else did I find in the drawers of my desk – the panniers of the patient donkey? Manuals that had barely been consulted, notebooks with nothing in them, and a handful of oddments which were best described as sentimental souvenirs. There was a flower from Green Park, for example, papery and crushed inside an envelope, and a tiny shard of masonry from a building site in the City; then there was a playing card with the word 'Magician' written on it in black felt-tip pen. And that was that.

My mind was now completely empty.

I mean, of course, there were little flurries of thought, like dry leaves blowing across the pavement at dusk, but the usual structure of my reasoning, imagination and feelings appeared to have seized up. *No more room.* I just sat there, listening to the freewheeling spool of the run film, as it were. I remember that I wondered whether this is what it felt like to be extremely old.

After a while – I don't know how long – I became aware of the drifting smoke from Kate's cigarette. We are not supposed to smoke in the office, and she had opened the window behind her; leaning back in her chair, with her feet propped up on an open drawer of her desk, she was gazing out at the neighbouring buildings, with her cigarette held just inches from her mouth.

It was one of the first evenings of the year when the daylight seems to linger. The sky was blue and clear and you could see the crescent of a new moon. Once again, I felt the call of an abstract kindness, made eloquent by the softness of the air, the gentle colour of the light, and the sense that whatever was composing these things was unconditionally benign. The image of grey eyes, filled with friendliness, came into my mind: *unimpeachable honesty!*

But when I looked again at the light in the streets, beyond Kate's profile, and felt again that strong pull, I suddenly knew that I was catching just the merest trace of some far greater kindness and unconditional love which was behind all of the love and the kindness and the unimpeachable honesty that I had ever seen or witnessed. That those manifestations – light, grey eyes, soft air – were simply the proof, by their very constitution, of the perfection of this greater source. *The bringer of cool water*: Claudia Cardinale in a café on Victoria Station, but that she, perfect as she seemed, was simply the ambassador, the angel, of this deeper sense that was calling – to me, personally – through Duke Street and Davies Street, in the blue evening light of early spring.

Trying to corner this sensation, I lost it, of course. Kate was still sitting by the window, and I had forgotten that she was there. We two were the only ones left in the office by now; the rest had gone down to the next floor, to the leaving party. Kate leaned to one side and flicked the ash off her cigarette into a plastic cup; it hissed as it hit the dregs of cold coffee. I sat up straight, wishing that I could reconnect with the feelings of the last few minutes.

I have never been any good at those cosy little chats which you're supposed to have with people in the office after there's been some sort of crisis. I never quite trust the friendliness which they generate; it always seems to be based on factioneering rather than affection. But looking at Kate, I did feel sorry for her. Her escapade with Simon Grinch had caused the equivalent of landing her on the front page of a newspaper under an embarrassing, crowing headline. And it was nobody else's business what they wanted to get up to.

You can't talk like that in the office, though. People would think you're just trying to be superior, or show the rest of them up. The only resistance is not to collaborate; and so I simply smiled across the room and said that I thought I'd join the others. Just then, Simon peered cautiously around the edge of the door, and that was my cue to leave. It's the wife I feel sorry for, I thought.

The corridor seemed bright and I suddenly realized that we'd been sitting in our office without any lights on. At the top of the stairs, I bumped into Potter, and he turned to speak with me. 'I think we ought to have a chat,' he said. 'Not now. Tomorrow.' And then he nodded, and carried on trotting downstairs, in his dynamic, energized way. Looking at the back of his head, I was suddenly glad that I hadn't hit him with the stapler.

These leaving parties are always peculiar, especially when one of the leavers is a lady in middle age, and the other is a reasonably young man, champion of champions amongst the good blokes. Frankie is short and heavily built, with curly fair hair, a red, plump face and little gold-framed glasses. He tends to have a constantly quizzical expression, as though he is permanently amazed by the irrationality of everything. This expression is backed up by his endless stream of sarcastic one-liners. He chews gum all the time, frowning and raising his eyebrows in time to his chewing, in a way which makes his whole face eloquent of his thought processes. As I walked into his crowded office, he was just leaning forward to drink from a pint glass filled with lager. He didn't see me, surrounded as he was by friends and well-wishers.

At the other end of the room, grouped around a pair of neat, tidied desks, Irene and her friends were sitting on typists' chairs, each with a paper plate in their laps, on which were modest slices of chocolate cake. Beside them, there were white plastic cups, carefully half filled with sparkling rosé. Perry caught my eye, and waved, his mouth full. He looked very tall in that particular gathering.

'D'you see Potter?' he asked. 'He was looking for you – again.'

I said that I'd seen him and that he wanted to have a meeting tomorrow. Perry must have guessed from my expression that I wasn't going to talk about my prospects at the office.

'D'you mind if I say something?' he went on. 'And I don't mean this in the wrong way . . .' – he started to laugh – 'but you're weird.'

And then he did laugh, and patted my arm as though to reassure me that he meant no offence. When I looked at him I could see that he was genuinely curious about me. Another few sentences down this conversation and he'd have started to become quite intimate, or confessional. I smiled, and offered an expression of mock alarm. Then I asked if I could get him a drink. He looked down at his plastic cup. 'Is there any more wine going?'

I turned away, threading through the little crowd towards the desk by the wall where the drinks were placed. The desk had been covered by a paper tablecloth, and about twelve bottles of the sparkling rosé were neatly arranged in one corner. On the other side, bottles of lager stood next to a brown bowl which was filled with peanuts.

I poured two glasses of wine, one for Perry and one for myself, and then I pushed back into the crowd, handing Perry his cup and saying 'Cheers' in his direction. And then I turned away again.

Had my feelings in the office, of sensing that greater kindness, been nothing more than the luxurious sentimentality of self-pity? The rosé was deliciously cold, but I only sipped at mine. I felt like I wanted cold water and fresh air. I could see Anne, chatting with Lampshade. Dave was in the middle of a heated discussion. He had stepped forward into the circle of drinkers, making his points with a jab of his finger, and then stepping back, throwing peanuts into his mouth. I put down my drink, no longer really wanting it, and looked once more around the room.

The voices and laughter were one loud noise by now. Thirty conversations were going on at once, cigarettes had been lit, the wine and beer were beginning to make people more generous, earnest or affable towards one another. The group around Frankie were particularly raucous, and as I looked over towards them – looking for something to hate, in fact – I found that I didn't want to hate them anymore.

My failure as an urban anthropologist had stemmed from the fact that I lacked the necessary detachment – or possessed the wrong kind of empathy – to remain at a distance from my subjects. My interest in status, image and appearance had always been fixated on myself, the more I resented the people around me. But looking at Frankie and his mates, as they clustered together, red faced and roaring, I suddenly felt that detachment – for the very first time, I think – and lost the reflex to hate. Perry's comment came back to me, 'You're weird.' Then I remembered that look in Ron Ryan's eyes, nearly twenty years ago, of slightly puzzled sadness.

It felt like it was time to leave. I didn't want to go across the road to the pub. The most important thing, as I took a last look around the room, at the men's grey-suited backs and the laughing women, was to defend the rare mood which my day had delivered: to test its strength in the walk to Victoria. I felt as though I was carrying tissue-thin crystal, which could yet turn out to be indestructible.

I made my way back to my own office. The corridors were quiet, and the offices were filled with that low humming sound of idling technology which you can only hear when the clamour of the working day is over. Cables, ducts and processors, generating an endless one movement symphony, played on one chord. At this time of day, when there are only a few people left in the office, all human noises seem much louder, too. The cleaners coming round with their tubular steel trolleys, and the clattering sound of fresh bin liners being unfurled; the pause in their progress, followed by a shouted greeting or a sudden burst of answering laughter to a comment you couldn't make out. Then the slow whine of a stiff hydraulic door hinge, and the clump of the heavy door, sounding so final.

Back in our office, the lights were still off and Kate and Simon were nowhere to be seen. The blue crates were still in the middle of the room, filled with our files and manuals and spreadsheets. I could even see the three squat binders of the Systems Amendment Sheets, poking up from the side of one crate. I looked at my own little desk – *patient donkey* – and thought how undefended it seemed.

In the darkness, the window frames were filled with the grey and orange of reflected street light; the upper-most panes were standing oblongs of vivid blue. It sounds really stupid, but I couldn't bring myself, yet, to look down into the streets – that vista of rooftops, stretching away towards Berkeley Square and Green Park, felt but invisible, beyond. I could still feel the tug of that promise of kindness; it was like the memory of love in a dream, the warmth of the smile, the blue of the bay.

I pulled on my raincoat and checked that I had left nothing behind. The office still looked much bigger than usual, as though its whole character had changed. It felt like there was space to breathe, that I could move freely, unstooped – my chest open, as they say. I listened to the sound of the room for a second, hearing that hum of technology as another person might listen to the sound of a sea wind, rustling through dune grass, and then I went back into the corridor.

The 18.38 train from Victoria is always crowded. I had a seat by the window, and because of the press of people I was leaning with the side of my head against the glass. The carriage was warm. It felt like body temperature, that kind of heat which makes you drowsy the moment you sit down. As the train slid out of the station, gaining once more the stark span of Grosvenor Bridge, I saw some high clouds, the colour of iron, pressing down on the blue of the evening light.

I closed my eyes, and saw the vastness of an empty beach at low tide. It looked the size of a desert. Only on the far horizon could you see the thin silver line of the sea, glinting in the late afternoon. And about halfway to that glistening line, adrift, as it were, in the immensity of the empty beach, were the splintering timbers of an old abandoned pier which stood alone, facing the open sky, redundant yet meaningful, like a structure left behind by an earlier civilization.

The train jolted, and I looked for a second at the backs of some houses, grey in the twilight. Before the warmth of sleep pulled me back, I wanted to remember that colour of the light: a light which promised love, and which, knowing all the things which you know about yourself, would still love you, forever.

I must have been nine or ten years old when I ran

across the flattened, rippled sand on that lonely beach, thrilling to the splashes as my feet hit the tiny rivulets of sea water, left behind the tide. The old pier seemed enormous, close to – a high platform, with the blackened remains of rusted iron standards on either side, which had once held lamps. Beneath it were shallow pools of water, their surfaces quite still.

And it was there that I found what looked like hollow stones, no bigger than pebbles, but paper thin. They were slightly wedge-shaped at one end, and on their flattened, upper sides – their foreheads, if you like – were neatly curving patterns of the tiniest perforations. After I had crouched down to study them, daring myself to pick one up, and finding it dry and almost weightless, I had looked up again at the sky. And I imagined the blue rim of the atmosphere, and the beginnings of space, and how these were the skulls of aliens, to be laid very gently to rest.